CRITICAL ACCLAIM FOR

DELIRIUM *of the* BRAVE

"An ambitious *roman à clef* . . . enough whispered scandal . . . to keep the reading lamps burning late."
—*Publishers Weekly*

"An entertaining novel that effectively evokes a Savannah of another time."　　　　　　　—*Savannah Morning News*

"I'm not taking anything away from Mr. Berendt, but I personally believe that Dr. Harris's *DELIRIUM OF THE BRAVE* catches a lot more of the romance and intrigue that are the real heart of Savannah."
　—Regina Odom, Regina's Books and Cards, Savannah

"Old-fashioned multigenerational saga of buried treasure, hidden sin, and the redemptive power of religion and family, set in balmy Savannah. [An] ultimately uplifting reaffirmation of Southern gentility, fair play, and blind faith."
—*Kirkus Reviews*

"Five years after the best-selling phenomenon, *MIDNIGHT IN THE GARDEN OF GOOD AND EVIL*, the Old South is rising again. This time, the title is *DELIRIUM OF THE BRAVE. DELIRIUM* . . . delivers in generous portions those things the South is known for and that Southerners love to see in themselves: the noble gesture, pride, honor, good manners, storied family histories, the romance of the Lost Cause . . . [and] offers a peek ░░░░░░ ░░░ gh the gauze of fiction. It's a st░░░░░░░░░░░░░░░░░░ realness—and that well-░░░░░░░░░░░░░░░░░░░░░░ogy."
　　　　　　　　　　　　　　　　　—░░*Union-Tribune*

DELIRIUM
of the BRAVE

WILLIAM CHARLES
HARRIS, JR.

St. Martin's Paperbacks

Previously published by Frederic C. Beil, Publisher, Inc.

"September 1913," by W. B. Yeats, courtesy of Simon & Schuster Inc.

DELIRIUM OF THE BRAVE

Copyright © 1998 by William Charles Harris, Jr.

ISBN: 0-312-97713-1

Printed in the United States of America

St. Martin's Press hardcover edition / November 1999
St. Martin's Paperbacks edition / October 2001

St. Martin's Paperbacks are published by St. Martin's Press, 175 Fifth Avenue, New York, NY 10010.

10 9 8 7 6 5 4 3 2 1

FOR

MY FATHER, WHO SHOWED ME HOW
MY MOTHER, WHO TAUGHT ME WHY
AND
MY WIFE, WHO INSPIRED ME

SEPTEMBER 1913

What need you, being come to sense,
But fumble in a greasy till
And add the halfpence to the pence
And prayer to shivering prayer, until
You have dried the marrow from the bone;
For men were born to pray and save:
Romantic Ireland's dead and gone,
It's with O'Leary in the grave.

Yet they were of a different kind,
The names that stilled your childish play,
They have gone about the world like wind,
But little time had they to pray
For whom the hangman's rope was spun,
And what, God help us, could they save?
Romantic Ireland's dead and gone,
It's with O'Leary in the grave.

Was it for this the wild geese spread
The grey wing upon every tide;
For this that all that blood was shed,
For this Edward Fitzgerald died,
And Robert Emmet and Wolfe Tone,
All that delirium of the brave?
Romantic Ireland's dead and gone,
It's with O'Leary in the grave.

Yet could we turn the years again,
And call those exiles as they were
In all their loneliness and pain,
You'd cry, 'Some woman's yellow hair
Has maddened every mother's son':
They weighed so lightly whay they gave.
But let them be, they're dead and gone,
They're with O'Leary in the grave.

—W. B. YEATS

CONTENTS

DELIRIUM
of the BRAVE

PROLOGUE

The Grand Dragon of the Invisible Empire watched from his hiding place among the palmettos as the *Admiral Graf Spee* rounded the last curve in the creek and inched up to the old earthen pier built by the Confederates in 1864. Two of his sons stood tensely by his side, watching the five men on the boat unload their supplies.

The Grand Dragon stood dead still; the early morning sun glistened off a paste of mucous draining from his nostrils, painting his upper lip. Occasionally his tongue darted up to lick some of the mucous before it stretched out in long silvery strings and splattered on the dried palmetto fronds at his feet. His bead-bright eyes watched every movement of the five men carrying their gear along the pier to the base of the big live oak at the island's edge. The Grand Dragon cocked his head slightly and snorted softly to himself, straining to pick up their words.

In the cover of the dense underbrush the Grand Dragon's breath frosted in the cold March air when he grunted the order to return to the hiding place deep within the dense twists of thick vines and thorny brush that darkened the northern two-thirds of Raccoon Island. As he left, he turned for one more look at the intruders, especially the big black one. Then in a primitive sign of ownership, he urinated where he stood, marking his property. His sons could smell the pungent odor as the vapor from the yellow pool burned the still morning air. The Grand Dragon was the master of all that he surveyed. These intruders from the mainland would tarry only briefly in his kingdom, or regret their invasion.

After camp was set up, the intruders gathered limbs fallen from the grand oak whose branches shadowed the entire campsite. Soon, busy flames whipped and curled around the wood and took the chill off the air. The men stood around the fire and warmed themselves as they talked of this last attempt to find the Driscoll treasure.

They were all in their fiftieth year. And all, except for Vinnie from South Philly, had been born and reared in Savannah. As young boys the four Savannahians had come to Raccoon Island regularly—three in search of the Driscoll treasure and one to tend the grave of his war-hero great-grandfather. It had been thirty-two years since they had been on Raccoon Island and seen the remains of the old fort called Battery Jasper.

"So, Lloyd," said Vinnie in his harsh South Philadelphia accent, "John-Morgan tells me your great-grandfather and his great-grandfather were killed here during the Civil War and they took the secret of the Driscoll treasure with them?"

Lloyd Bryan looked at John-Morgan Hartman and smiled. Then Lloyd looked into the fire. "Yeah, they died in each other's arms. There were about a dozen witnesses. My great-granddaddy Shadrack was a slave who belonged to Captain Patrick Driscoll, John-Morgan's great-granddaddy. Some say they buried everything the family owned to keep it from Sherman. As the story goes, they got killed together before they could get word back to the family where it was buried."

"You think it's true, John-Morgan?" asked Vinnie.

John-Morgan shrugged. "I used to. My mamma thinks it's true. I just don't know anymore. I've been thinking about it for a long time. Maybe we should call it the 'legend' of the Driscoll treasure. We dug this whole island up over the years, and all we could find were cannon balls and rusty nails. But we think we've got it narrowed down to a fairly small area. It's the only place we never looked when we were kids."

Bubba Silverman walked over to the picnic table and spread out the map that John-Morgan had made of Raccoon Island back when they were boys. Though yellow and torn at the edges, it was very detailed. Every place they had searched for the treasure over the years was carefully marked.

"This is where we think it might be," said Bubba, pointing to an area on the map in which "Der Schwarzwald" was carefully printed in Gothic letters.

"Schwarzwald," said Vinnie. "Isn't that the German for Black Forest?"

"That's exactly what it means," said Mike Sullivan. Mike leaned over the map and smiled, recalling all the good times they had had on Raccoon Island looking for the Driscoll treasure.

"Why do you call it that?" asked Vinnie.

"Cause it's deep and dark and scary as hell," said Mike as he ran his hand caressingly over the map.

"What's so scary about some damn woods? You guys think there's spooks in there or something?" Vinnie was grinning, but nobody else shared in the joke.

"It's so scary that we never dared to go into it when we were kids," said John-Morgan. "There's something terrible in there. Something that could tear your ass up in a heartbeat."

"Aw, come on now, don't think ya gonna jerk around this dumb-shit Yankee from the big city. I been around too." Vinnie was still grinning.

"We're not kidding at all, Vinnie," said Lloyd. "That's what we got the guns for."

Finally the grin faded, for two very good reasons. First, Lloyd didn't act as if he were trying to yank Vinnie around. And second, Lloyd was a Catholic priest. Vinnie had never known a priest to lie.

Standing alone, a few feet away from the rest of the group, Vinnie was overcome with an odd, strangely exciting emotion. Maybe they weren't kidding him after all.

"So, ah, just wha'cha call this here, ah, 'thing' ya been talking about?" he asked after a moment.

As one, the four men looked up from the map. There was a moment of silence. Then Lloyd spoke for the group.

"We call him the Grand Dragon. He probably knows we're here already."

"The what?"

"We call him the Grand Dragon of Raccoon Island," repeated Lloyd without expression.

I

THE CONQUERED BANNER

Was it for this the wild geese spread
The grey wing upon every tide

Furl that banner, softly, slowly!
Treat it gently—it is holy—
For it droops above the dead.
Touch it not—unfold it never.
Let it droop there, furled forever,
For its people's hopes are dead!

—THE LAST VERSE OF "THE CONQUERED
BANNER" BY FATHER ABRAM RYAN, POET
LAUREATE OF THE CONFEDERATE STATES OF
AMERICA

It can also be used to get distinct echoes from trees a foot in diameter, and other objects can be located in the same way. A good technique for a beginner is to sweep slowly back and forth with the clicker while operating it at a rate of one or two clicks per second. A few minutes of careful listening will show that much can be learned about objects of this general size, provided that they are at a sufficient distance to yield an echo which is clearly separate from the emitted click itself. Experience will show that echoes are most easily recognized when only one large echoing surface is within range. Several trees in a courtyard surrounded by large buildings give multiple echoes that only careful scanning can resolve.

Before very long your hands become cramped from the unnatural position in which they must be held in order both to operate the clicker and provide it with a horn. It is not difficult to mount the clicker in a small horn made of cardboard, light metal, or plastic. While a parabolic shape is perhaps ideal, a fairly deep cone will serve fairly well. The most important point is to provide a means of bending the dented sheet of steel back and forth without having any opening at the back of the horn through which the click can reach the user's ears directly at a high level of intensity. One device of this sort is shown in Fig. 7.

After you have learned to detect trees and houses by hearing their echoes, you will find it worth while to experiment with an easily recognized target such as a building. Keep moving closer as you click. If you find it difficult to be sure whether you are really hearing echoes, it may be helpful to try using the clicker while blindfolded or with your eyes closed. You will then be in much the same situation as a blind man trying to find his way about by means of echoes. Many blind people have

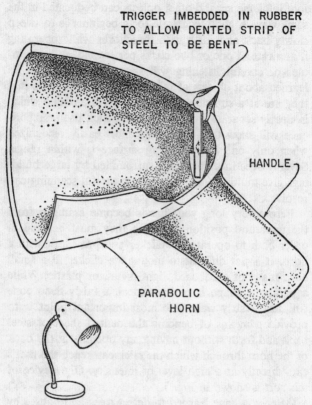

TRIGGER IMBEDDED IN RUBBER
TO ALLOW DENTED STRIP OF
STEEL TO BE BENT

HANDLE

PARABOLIC
HORN

Fig. 7. A very satisfactory device for echo experiments can be made like this. The inside of the horn should be a paraboloid of revolution, and the clicker must be mounted at the focal point of the parabola. The Fiberglas and plastic boat- or car-patching materials laid on a plaster of Paris form make excellent horns, and so do the parabolic reflectors of certain desk lamps.

learned to do this with great skill and success. As you walk toward a building from 15–25 meters away, the echo of the clicker is at first clearly separated from the original click but gradually merges with it until there is only one sound as best you can tell. At this point you should turn in some other direction, where no large object will return echoes, and operate the clicker several times. The clicks will sound different, and if in doubt you can alternately point toward the building and then in some other direction. After this difference has been recognized, you can move in closer to the building, repeatedly clicking both toward it and away in non-echoing directions. It is surprising how close you can come and still be clearly aware of a difference in the sound of the clicker when it is pointed toward and away from the wall. At very close range, less than 10 feet for example, the difference will begin to be one of loudness; the echoes are of sufficient intensity that they add appreciably to the click with which they are fused. This is why the horn is so important to shield you from the direct sound; if the horn could be perfect, so that *all* the sound energy of the clicker traveled away from you, then the echoes would become unmistakable.

It is helpful to digress at this point into a little thought about the wave lengths of audible sounds and the relationship of these wave lengths to the practicable size for a horn to direct the click forward. It is a general property of wave motion that specular (that is, mirror-like) reflections can be obtained only from objects that are larger than one wave length. Water waves on the surface of a ripple tank or a bathtub can be reflected from the edges of the tank or tub or from objects several centimeters long. Such reflections obey the same rules as those that hold for light waves; for instance, the angle of reflection from a plane surface equals the angle of incidence. But quite different results are observed if the object reflecting the waves is only one wave length or less. Then one sees secondary waves which may be called echoes radiating in many directions from the small object. The strength of the echo waves in different directions varies in a complicated way, both with the shape of the object and particularly with its size, relative to the wave length. In fact, if the object is much smaller than one wave length, its shape makes almost no difference at all. Later on I shall describe some simple experiments with the clicker by which one can see how these same rules apply to audible sound waves. When the echoes travel in many directions from an object which itself is small compared to the wave length, they are often called *scattered* rather than reflected sound.

But we started this digression to consider how the wave length of the click would affect the usefulness of a horn to direct the sound straight forward. A horn is a special kind of acoustic mirror, and for this purpose we want one shaped so that sound waves generated somewhere inside will all be reflected from the horn's surfaces, reinforcing each other and coming out of the mouth as parallel wave fronts traveling in the same direction. If the sound is generated at a point, the most effective horn to concentrate the sound waves into one direction will be one with a parabolic shape. This means that if you cut the horn longitudinally, any section will be a parabola with the sound source at its focus. One of the geometrical properties of a parabola is that any line radiating from the focus will strike the surfaces of the parabola at such an angle that when reflected (at an angle equal to the angle of incidence) it will be parallel to the axis of the parabola.

This sounds rather complicated, but perhaps Fig. 8 will help to make it clear. Really this is a very familiar

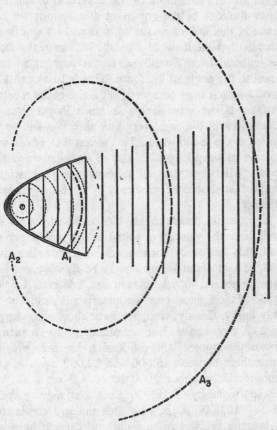

Fig. 8. When the wave length is larger than the mouth of the horn, as in the low-frequency sound waves A_1, A_2, and A_3, there is little or no focusing. But with a much smaller wave length a narrow beam of plane waves is produced.

story, for searchlights, flashlights, and automobile head-lights are all made more or less according to this prin-ciple. But one of the important assumptions we have made in this line of reasoning is that the sound waves generated at the focus of a parabolic horn really would be reflected from the surface of the horn at an angle equal to the angle of incidence. This is true only if the wave length is short compared to the size of the reflecting surface. If the wave length is much longer than the dimensions of the horn, very little direction will be im-parted to the sound waves. This means that a horn must be several wave lengths in size to do what we want it to do. What does this tell us about the frequencies of sound that should be produced by an echo-generating clicker?

Suppose we decide to use 256 sound waves per sec-ond. Since the velocity of sound is 344 meters per sec-ond, this frequency corresponds to a wave length of 344/256, or about 1.3 meters. To be effective, our horn must be several wave lengths in size, and even if it were made of the lightest possible materials it would be un-duly bulky. Clearly, then, we want short wave lengths or high frequencies. But we cannot go to frequencies above the upper limits of human hearing, which is somewhere between 15,000 and 20,000 c.p.s. A good compromise is about 5000 to 10,000 c.p.s. A wave whose frequency is 10,000 c.p.s. has a wave length of 344/10,000 meters, or a little under 3 centimeters. It is quite practicable to build and carry a horn sev-eral centimeters in size, and if this were the only consideration we would choose the highest frequencies or shortest wave lengths that were easily audible. Bats use frequencies up to 130,000 c.p.s. with wave lengths down to 2.5 millimeters, and their tiny mouths or ears can concentrate these short sound waves quite effectively. The toy clicker produces a number of frequencies or wave lengths within each brief click, but it would require much more complicated click generators to produce an ideal click containing only a single frequency and a pulse short enough in duration to yield echoes distinctly separate from the original. Indeed, this consideration of separateness itself imposes limits on the possible frequencies. Several waves are necessary to establish a clear frequency, and if our sound is to last only 1 millisecond it can contain only 10 waves of 10,000 c.p.s., or 5 waves of 5000 c.p.s.

What I have been suggesting in these simple experiments with a clicker is to act as though you were blind and see what you can discover about the larger objects in your surroundings solely by means of echoes. Later on I shall discuss in more detail what blind people actually do and the success they have achieved as well as the limitations that seem to prevent echolocation from warning them about all the major obstacles that threaten their safe progress. But before turning to this direct application to a pressing problem of a large group of handicapped persons, we will find it helpful to consider certain physical properties of echoes that determine their strength and audibility. For this purpose we can make good use of both real echoes from a clicker and "echoes" in the ripple tank, which is so useful in the physics laboratory for the analysis of wave motion.

The Velocity of Sound Measured by Means of Echoes

As a beginning we may consider a simple method of determining the approximate velocity of sound by an extension of the already-mentioned procedure of timing the return of an echo from a distant hillside. If the distance to the hill is not known and if the travel time of the sound and its echo is a few seconds, a good stop watch (which can measure time to a tenth of a second) would allow us to determine the distance to the hill, if we assume that we know the velocity of sound. Or if we know the distance, we can use the same time measurement to estimate the velocity at which the sound waves travel. If the basic limit of accuracy in our time measurement is determined by the stop watch at 0.1 second, the uncertainty in our measurement of distance would be the distance over which sound travels in that interval of time, or approximately 34 meters. But this would be the round-trip distance, so that theoretically we could measure the distance to the hill with an accuracy of ± 17 meters. Another uncertainty is the human reaction time, the interval between the actual arrival of a sound and the pressing of the button on the stop watch. While this is an appreciable fraction, certainly more than 0.1 of a second, there is not likely to be a great difference between the first reaction time to the original sound and the reaction time in stopping the watch when one hears the echo; hence they will nearly cancel each other. Another error is likely to occur if the emitted sound and the echo build up gradually. If a half second is needed to reach maximum sound intensity, and if the echo is enough fainter so that only the peak value is audible, then we will probably find that the stop watch is pressed one reaction time after the very beginning of the outgoing sound, but not until one reaction time after the echo is nearly at its peak. This can easily cause an error of about 0.3 second unless a very sharp sound is used for the experiment.

A similar experiment can be performed with the clicker, provided it can be operated fairly rapidly. Suppose you stand 30 meters from a large building and point the clicker so that a distinct echo is heard. Since the sound travels 60 meters from clicker to building and back to your ears, this trip will require 60/344, or about 0.17 second. If you operate the clicker twice per second, you will hear an outgoing click at a time you may designate as zero, an echo at 0.17 second, a second emitted click at 0.50 second, a second echo at 0.67 second, etc. If we speed up our operation of the clicker, the second click will eventually come at 0.17 second and so will mask the echo. If we can operate the clicker with sufficient regularity, this fusion of echo with second click provides another way to measure distance—provided we know the velocity of sound. A mechanical device such as a metronome can control the rate of clicking more precisely, but with a little practice a good approximation can be achieved. One practical difficulty is that the click made by bending the strip of steel will usually be slightly louder or different in quality from that made when the strip is unbent. Thus successive clicks alternate in level or quality, and it is not always easy to maintain an even rhythm. But it can be done and, regardless of its practicability, it is worth while to understand this simple method for estimating distance by the rate of clicking necessary to cause each echo to fuse with the following click. One effective way to estimate the critical rate is to have someone else count the number of clicks in a 5- or 10-second period measured with a stop watch or the second hand of an ordinary watch.

The same clicker may also be used to demonstrate convincingly the concentration of echoes into certain directions when they have been reflected from surfaces of various sizes relative to the wave lengths in the click. Most toy clickers have a frequency range between 3 and 10 kilocycles, so that the most intense sound waves have wave lengths of a few centimeters. When such wave lengths strike the wall of a building, they are reflected almost exactly as light waves would be from a mirror. If the clicker is pointed directly at the wall, the echo will come straight back, but if the emitted sound strikes ob-

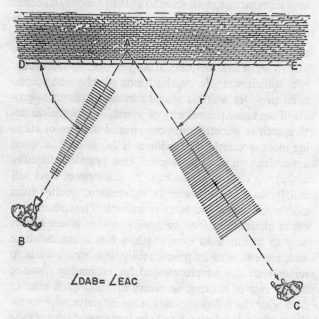

$\angle DAB = \angle EAC$

Fig. 9. The law of reflection describes the way in which sound reflects from a large flat surface. When making this experiment, observe the relative positions of the two boys.

liquely, the echoes will rebound away from the clicker, as indicated in Fig. 9. This is why it is so easy to locate a building by scanning with the clicker; the echo is far louder when the horn is pointed straight at the wall. Two people can co-operate in a simple experiment that demonstrates how these echoes behave. One should aim the clicker at the wall 20° to 30° to one side of a perpendicular from clicker to wall, while the second listens for the echo. He will not hear it so clearly if he stands beside the clicker at point B as he will if he walks to one side and a little behind the clicker to a point such as C. The position where the echo is loudest can be predicted on the same principle that governs the specular reflection of light from mirrors; namely, that the angle of reflection, r (angle EAC), equals the angle of incidence, i (angle DAB). This experiment will give clearer results if the listener stands a little behind the clicker, so that he is shielded from the direct, outgoing click by the horn. The same experiment can be performed more accurately by mounting the clicker on a camera tripod and turning it slowly to different angles relative to the wall. The listener may then move back and forth until he finds the points where he hears the echo most clearly. Or the listener may stand still in various positions while the first person turns the clicker slowly back and forth from right to left according to his instructions. It is remarkable how well the results of such experiments confirm the rule that the angle of reflection equals the angle of incidence.

There is an entirely different situation in which it is easy to experience a simple type of echolocation. When you ride in an automobile, sitting by an open window, you hear a number of sounds from the engine, the tires, and the rush of air past the window. As you drive past a high stone wall, through an underpass, or close to any large surface, these sounds will change in quality. A series of concrete guardrail posts, the masonry posts used to support iron fences, or even a row of wooden fence posts can be detected from a rapid series of swishing sounds as the car moves by. Try listening with your eyes closed as you ride along some familiar route and you may be surprised to find how many places you can recognize by ear. If you find a series of clearly "audible" fence posts, compare their sound effects with those you hear in passing through an underpass. Along the posts it is primarily the high frequencies that return as echoes from the relatively small surfaces; in the underpass almost the whole range of sounds of the car will be reflected from the large wall surface. If you make a careful study of these sounds while your car is driven at about the same speed, you will find that you can learn to recognize many types of structures, such as parked cars, from the echoes which they add to the roughly constant sounds made by your own car.

Echoes are used by bats and men to locate smaller and more elusive objects than the walls of buildings, and some interesting properties of reflected waves become important once we begin to work with smaller objects. After you have acquired some experience with the clicker, it is of interest to try it on trees, telephone poles, or other objects that can easily be found out in the open away from other echo-making objects. With care and practice you can detect trees as small as 6 inches from several feet away, and when this has been accomplished, you can again call upon another person to point the clicker at the tree while you, the listening observer, move about to different positions to find where the echo sounds loudest. The result will usually be that the echo can be heard over a much wider range of angles than happened with the louder echo from a building. This is because the tree is only a little more than one wave length in diameter and the echoes are spread over a much wider range of directions, as indicated in Fig. 10. Just as a horn less than one wave length in size fails to concentrate sound, small objects scatter their echoes. If you can hear echoes from trees or poles as small

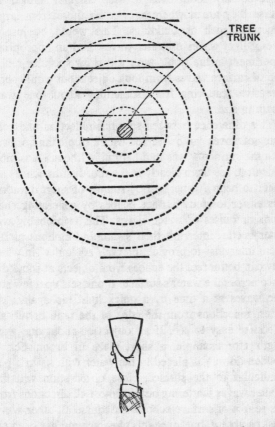

Fig. 10. When the wave length is greater than the size of the object (here a tree trunk), the echo, or scattered sound moves out in all directions. The solid lines indicate the original sound, the dashed lines the echoes, and the width of the lines the intensity of sound.

as one or two wave lengths, you will find them almost equally loud over a wide angular range. Of course they are nowhere as loud as those from larger structures such as buildings. This would be just as true of light waves or water waves, and an appropriate experiment in the ripple tank will show specular reflection of surface waves from long objects but would show extensive scattering from something about one wave length in size.

This difference between specular reflection and scattering of waves can be studied with a ripple tank or even with the surface waves in a bathtub, although it is more difficult to see them clearly in the tub. Just as echoes are easier to hear if generated by sounds of short duration, it is easier to study surface echoes by generating short trains or pulses of water waves. This is probably why water beetles interrupt their swimming motions at frequent intervals—to provide intervals of "quiet" in which they can better feel the echoes from objects at some distance across the water's surface. If one sets up a few surface waves at a time by a quick light tap against the water, reflections from the edge of the tank or tub are of course easy to see. If an object of about one wave length (for example, a short piece of broomstick or wooden dowel) is placed in the water with its axis perpendicular to the surface, close observation will find smaller waves scattering out in almost all directions from this source of surface echoes. Of course all other waves must be absent, but, once this phenomenon has been observed, it is of some interest to vary the size of the cylindrical object from the smallest that produces visible scattered waves up to sizes well in excess of one wave length. Such experiments convince one of the real difference between sharply directional specular reflection and the diffuse scattering from small echo sources. These two general types of echoes will be important when we move on from the physics of echoes to a study of the actual uses to which they are put by blind men and by the bats and other animals which have developed such refined and precise methods of echolocation for the carrying out of their daily business.

CHAPTER 4

The Language of Echoes

From our brief, qualitative look at the remarkable navigational feats of some animals, it seemed clear that sound was a most important message carrier. This led us to a detailed examination of sound itself, particularly how it echoes or reflects, in order that we might experiment more skillfully and intelligently in an attempt to learn how echoes are actually used by animals—what are their limits, what aids or hinders, what physical characteristics are especially suited to echolocation, what are the special characteristics of the sounds these animals make. We may hope to discover some important bits of evidence, perhaps obscure at the moment, which will aid blind people in their travels, and even if this does not occur, we will certainly know our environment better. Men have always learned from animals, and even in this age of electronics and atomic structure we still have much to learn. Since the bats are so expert in the use of echoes, let us begin by examining in more detail the sounds they broadcast to produce the echoes which guide their agile flight.

Orientation Sounds of Bats

Bats make a variety of vocal sounds; for example, when disturbed they squeak and chitter. But we are interested primarily in the sounds they use in flight to generate useful echoes that tell them about objects at some distance. These *orientation sounds* are all of high frequency, though they overlap slightly the range of human hearing to produce the very faint audible ticking we have discussed. But most of the sound energy emitted by flying bats lies at frequencies from 10 to 150 kc in different species, and I will describe only one or two examples of orientation sounds that have been measured from a few typical kinds of bats.

One of the simplest acoustic patterns is that used by the *horseshoe bats,* an insectivorous group that lives in Europe, Asia, Australia, and Africa. They use orientation sounds of nearly a single frequency, which may be anywhere from 60 to 120 kc, depending on the species. The individual sounds last only a small fraction of a second, usually from 50 to 100 milliseconds, but this is much longer than the duration of other bats' sounds. The name horseshoe bat refers to a complicated series of folds or membranes surrounding the nostrils and the mouth with two roughly concentric rosettes which vaguely resemble a horseshoe when viewed from in front. The German zoologist Franz P. Moehres has shown recently that the horseshoe serves as a small horn to concentrate the emitted sound into a narrow beam which is swept back and forth as the bat scans its surroundings. Bats have a habit of hanging head downward by the hind feet, and the horseshoe bats have especially flexible hip joints. They can pivot through almost a complete circle as they scan with their beam of high-frequency sound. Often they dart out from such a position to seize an insect that flies within range.

Another group of bats, confined to the tropics, feed mostly upon fruit, but some also eat insects, which they may pick off the vegetation. These bats emit much fainter sounds than the horseshoe bats—extremely brief clicks, lasting from a fraction of a millisecond to 2 or 3 milliseconds. The sound waves making up these very short pulses are complicated, with a variety of frequencies from as low as 10 to as high as 150 kc, again depending on the species. The vampire bats, which feed on the blood of living animals and men, belong to this group. Without causing the victim to awake from his sleep, they feed by making small cuts with their very sharp teeth and drinking the blood that flows for a time before clotting. All these bats seem to refrain from the active pursuit of flying insects, and the intensity level of their sounds is so low that only the best of microphones and sound-analyzing equipment will register them. They may be called *whispering bats* to distinguish them from the other two groups.

The third major category includes the common insectivorous bats that are well known in North America and Europe. With a very few exceptions, these bats all hunt flying insects in the open, tracking their elusive moving prey on the wing, maneuvering through complicated split-second turns and other acrobatics to follow and intercept the erratic flight of moths and flying beetles, May flies and mosquitoes. The sounds used by this group, only a few milliseconds in duration and almost as intense as those of the horseshoe bats, have a characteristic frequency pattern. Each orientation sound starts at a very high frequency and drops rapidly during its brief life, to end about an octave below the frequency at which it started. The common little brown bats of the

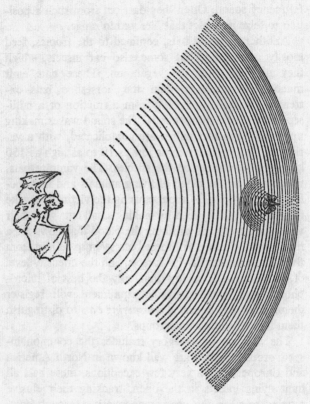

Fig. 11. The frequency and wave length of a bat's sound vary during each chirp. This diagram, which is approximately to scale, illustrates the small amount of sound reflected by one insect.

United States begin each of their orientation sounds at about 90 kc and end at 45 kc. Since each sound lasts only about 2 milliseconds, this is a very rapid change in frequency; indeed, this bat sweeps through a frequency band double the whole range of the human ear in 2 milliseconds. As illustrated in Fig. 11, a typical orientation sound contains only about 50 sound waves, no two exactly alike. The wave length of the initial waves is only half the wave length of those making up the end of the emitted sound. These sounds are *chirps,* at least that is what we call audible sounds made by certain insects when they sweep through as wide a range of frequencies within a fraction of a second. This type is sometimes called a frequency-modulated pulse of sound, and this group of bats may be thought of as "FM bats" in contrast to the horseshoe bats with their much longer, sharply beamed tones of nearly constant frequency, and the faint but complex clicks of the tropical "whispering bats."

Echoes of Insect Prey

The FM or chirping bats have been studied much more thoroughly than the other two groups; therefore, more is known about them. They seem to be the most highly specialized for a life of flight, very expert at maneuvering under the most difficult conditions. The daily (or nightly) business of catching insect food compels them to be highly skilled in the detection of such small moving objects and in the aerial acrobatics necessary to intercept them. Since bats do almost all their hunting on dark nights, often approaching insects from above or in wooded areas where they would have to be seen against a dark background, visual detection must be impossible. And Spallanzani, as we have said in Chapter 1, showed before 1800 that blind bats catch as many insects as normal animals. It has usually been thought that they located insects by listening for the sounds of their wingbeats, and this probably does occur in some circumstances when the flying insects make appreciable humming or buzzing noises. But I have discovered in recent years that the orientation sounds, the high-frequency chirps of these bats, are repeated at remarkably high rates as the bats locate and close in upon flying insects. Furthermore, bats will often pursue imitation insects such as pebbles or little wads of wet absorbent cotton tossed gently into the air as they fly by. They do not actually bite or swallow such decoys, but they swoop avidly towards them with the same increase in the tempo of the orientation sounds they employ when chasing real insects under natural conditions. When one realizes how silent are many of the small insects upon which bats feed, it becomes rather likely, though not rigorously proven, that the bats detect at least some of their insect prey by hearing echoes of their own chirps bouncing off the insects rather than relying solely on the sounds emitted by the insects themselves.

I shall return a little later to the patterns in which these orientation sounds are broadcast under various conditions, including the pursuit of insect prey. But first let us consider the effectiveness of the process of insect hunting. Just how many insects does a bat catch in a given time? How big are the insects caught? At what distances are they detected? Only very recently have we been able to provide even partial and tentative answers to such questions. Spallanzani and others who examined the stomachs of bats just returned from a night's hunting have marveled at the relatively large mass of finely chewed insect remains present in the digestive tract of every successful bat. One study showed that little brown bats weighing 7 grams commonly catch 1 gram of insects per hour of active hunting. Very recently we have been able to persuade a few bats to hunt insects in a laboratory flight room where the process could be studied and photographed. One smaller relative of the little brown bat, weighing only 3.5 grams, caught mosquitoes at such a rapid rate before our very eyes that after 15 minutes' hunting its weight had increased by 10 per cent to 3.85 grams. These particular mosquitoes weighed about 0.002 gram each. The bat had no possible way of gaining weight during these 15 minutes of closely observed hunting, aside from the weight of the mosquitoes caught. It drank no water and ate nothing else. It probably *lost* a little weight by the evaporation of water while breathing; therefore, it caught more than 0.35 gram of mosquitoes.

Dividing the weight gain by the weight of a single mosquito shows that at least 175 mosquitoes were caught in 15 minutes, or more than one every 6 seconds. This was also approximately the number of obvious mosquito-chasing maneuvers that we could count during this hunting spree. There is every reason to believe that similar rates of insect capture are commonplace events in the nightly activities of millions of these bats and their relatives all over the world. Of course, it is not always mosquitoes that are eaten; almost any kind of insect that is locally available and is not too big seems welcome. Sometimes moths up to an inch in wingspread are taken, but at other times these bats capture insects much smaller than mosquitoes. In one instance a small gnat weighing only 0.0002 gram was found still unswallowed in the mouth of a bat killed while it was hunting.

This maneuvering to capture one insect every 6 seconds is what makes the flight of bats appear so erratic. Far from being feeble fliers buffeted about by air currents, they are expert fliers engaging in the difficult interception of flying insects. Their percentage of successes must be very high indeed. Certainly they are doing vastly better than simply flying around with their mouths open. Even when mosquitoes are particularly abundant, their density is such that one of these small bats would have to fly all night before its mouth encountered a single mosquito purely by chance. Yet the actual rate of capture is one every few seconds.

Photographs of the bat pursuing an insect show that they sometimes begin their maneuvers when 2 or 3 feet from a mosquito. The pattern of the orientation sounds begins to change a fraction of a second before the bat turns toward its victim. The implications of these observations can be understood after a brief explanation of the rate at which a bat's frequency-modulated chirps are repeated during various types of flight. When a little brown bat is flying fairly straight and is not close to anything of immediate concern, it repeats its 1- to 2-millisecond chirps at rates of 10 to 20 per second. But whenever it approaches any small obstacles, such as wires stretched across a laboratory room to test its skill, many more chirps are emitted in a given interval of time. For brief periods the repetition rate may rise as high as 250 per second. When this happens, the individual chirps become shorter, usually less than 1 millisecond, so that silent intervals still exist between chirps. When the high-frequency sounds of these bats are studied under natural conditions, a clear distinction between straight and level flight and the active pursuit of flying insects becomes apparent. Such eavesdropping is only possible, of course, when we have apparatus which will detect the bat sounds that are inaudible. In one convenient form this apparatus "translates" each of the bat's high-frequency sounds into audible clicks in earphones or a small loudspeaker. This makes it possible to watch the bat while at the same time "listening" to its orientation sounds in this transposed form. Most of the details, such as the octave of frequency modulation, are lost, but there is one click from the loudspeaker every time the bat broadcasts one of its high-frequency chirps.

When this "listening" apparatus is used in some spot where bats do their insect hunting, we notice that one cruising past on a straight course several feet above the ground sounds like the slow putt-putt-putt-putt of a lazy, old gasoline engine. Often it will fly straight past with little or no change in this rhythm, but if its attention is attracted either to a real insect or to a decoy, such as a pebble tossed up in front of it, then there is a marked increase in the rate of the orientation sounds. Sometimes this is a slight increase in rate, but if the pursuit is serious, involving drastic maneuvers such as sudden turns, wingovers, or sharp dives, then the translation resembles the acceleration of a motorcycle engine. On occasion it rises to a real crescendo with the individual clicks coming so close together that for human ears they fuse into a whining buzz reminiscent of a chain saw. Such crescendos occur just when the bat is closing in on an elusive moving target, strong evidence against the idea that all location and tracking are done simply by listening to the sounds of the insect's wingbeats. In this case one would expect the bat to keep relatively quiet when near an insect so as to hear the faint buzzing of the insect's wings. Instead it fills the air with an extremely rapid series of chirps that would seem to interfere severely with any process of passive listening.

Precision of Echolocation

Another important aspect of bats' use of echoes for rapid and precise navigation is the small size of objects which can be detected and the distances at which detection can occur. The only feasible tests yet devised have involved wires or strings rather than small isolated ob-

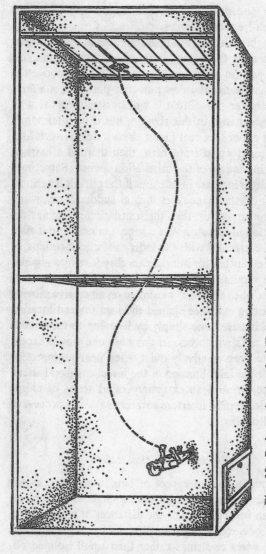

Fig. 12. Bat's navigational skill is tested in this room which is about 10 meters long and 3 meters wide. One row of wires is in the middle of the room and the second row is about 45 centimeters from the end wall.

jects like insects or pebbles. It is simply too difficult to keep small particles stationary in the air long enough to make accurate tests of bats' ability to dodge them. When wires are strung across a laboratory "flight" room, on the other hand, as diagramed in Fig. 12, the animals seem anxious to avoid collisions, although the brown bats weigh so little that they do not seem to be injured even in an occasional head-on crash against a taut wire.

When the wires are spaced 30 centimeters apart, or slightly more than the wingspread of the little brown bat, they make a difficult barrier that even the most skillful animals brush against lightly from time to time. The wires can be made smaller and smaller, without any marked effect on the percentage of misses registered by a really skillful animal, down to a wire diameter of a fraction of a millimeter. To be sure, many bats will be found on first testing in such an obstacle course to be clumsy, striking even the larger wires, but this is usually because they are in poor condition or not completely awakened from the deep sleep into which they lapse even on summer days. It is necessary to reduce the wire diameter to 0.07 millimeter (about the diameter of a human hair) before the little brown bats strike them at random. Even slightly larger wires, 0.12 millimeters in diameter, while difficult to miss, are dodged by the really skillful "athletes" among our experimental subjects far more often than one would expect.

Astonishing as it is that bats can detect wires as small as 0.12 millimeters, these previous experiments do not tell us at what distance this detection occurs. But motion pictures of the bats will give some indication of the range of detection when the translated orientation sounds are put on a sound track of the movie. Careful study of such movies, frame by frame, has enabled us to find the distance at which the rate of repetition of the bats' chirps first begins to increase. This varies from flight to flight, even for a single individual, but the average of numerous measurements with several sizes of wire gave the following results.

Diameter of wires (milli- meters)	Average rep. rate before approach to wires (pulses/sec)	Average maximum rep. rate (pulses/sec)	Average distance at which rep. rate first increases (centimeters)
3.0	12	50	215
1.07	12	40	185
0.65	13	30	150
0.46	13	40	120
0.28	12	27	105
0.18	12	22	90

These distances are considerably greater than one would guess from the bat's flight behavior. Ordinarily it flies along a fairly straight course and swerves only in the last few inches to avoid a wire. Yet the increasing pulse rate shows that it has already detected the wires and reacted to them at the distances shown in the table. If no wire is in place, there is no increase in the rate of the orientation chirps. Of course, a bat might be aware of the wires at still greater distances than the table shows, but it gives no sign of such awareness that we yet have learned to recognize. The important point is that even such small wires as those 0.18 millimeters in diameter are detected at some distance, not merely at the last possible moment to avoid collision. It is also interesting to note that small wires produce only a small increase in pulse rate. Actually the bat is moving so fast (approximately 4 meters per second) that with the smaller wires it often has time for only 2 or 3 additional pulses above the number it would have employed had there been no wire in place. All these facts testify that the echolocation practiced by bats is a refined, accurate method of orientation, not merely a crude sort of groping.

Bread upon the Waters

Nor do these examples by any means exhaust the list of difficult tasks which bats accomplish with some aid at least from echolocation. Certain of the whispering bats catch insects, small birds, or lizards that are resting on vegetation, but we are not sure that they do this by means of echolocation. They may simply listen to characteristic sounds coming from their prey. More amazing is the fact that four different species of the FM bats make their living by catching fish. This they do by flying just above the surface of the water and every now and then dipping their hind feet just below the surface. The claws on these feet are long, curved, and sharp, and the bats manage to gaff small minnows often enough to fill their stomachs every evening (as shown in Fig. 13). When fishing in this way on the darkest nights (and often with mist rising from the water), they emit a rapid series of chirps much like those of their insect-catching relatives. The gap between the two types of food gathering is not as great as it might at first seem, for the insectivorous bats drink by skimming the surface of the water and dipping their chins just deep enough to secure a drop of water at a time. This requires fine control, for a millimeter too deep would surely result in a dunking. These insectivorous bats also catch insects resting on the water surface, so perhaps it was a small step from this habit to reach for fish below the surface. In any event, the fish-catching species make much of their living in this way, and during their recent evolutionary history a relatively small anatomical adaptation has resulted in the specialized fish-gaffing claws.

When I have watched these bats in Panama, I have seen no sign that the fish were moving or disturbing the surface of the water in any way. Often it was glassy calm, and the bat flew for hundreds of feet a few inches above the surface, quickly lowering the hind feet into the water for a short distance and then raising them while continuing its low-altitude searching flight. How do these bats know where fish are to be captured? They are evi-

Fig. 13. Motion pictures of fishing bats actually gaffing minnows provided the model for this drawing. Prentice Bloedel took the photographs.

dently selective in their fishing, for they fly long distances just above the water and only rarely dip their claws beneath the surface. Since the fishing occurs on dark and misty nights, it is most unlikely that the fish could be seen and still less probable that they emit any sound audible to the bat flying in the air above the surface. Could it be that the fish-catching bats detect echoes from fish beneath the surface? At first glance this may seem only a slight modification of the process by which closely related bats catch insects in the air. But the physical discontinuity between air and water makes the transmission of sound difficult, and so echolocation seems an unlikely explanation.

As mentioned earlier in connection with the underwater hearing of fish and porpoises, sound waves have great difficulty in passing from air to water or vice versa. When airborne sound impinges on a smooth surface of water, with its direction of travel perpendicular to the water surface, only 0.12 per cent of the energy of the airborne sound continues beneath the surface as underwater sound waves. For a sound wave traveling from water to air, the same small fraction of the acoustic energy striking the surface from below continues outwards into the air. This means that a flying bat's orientation sounds striking the water, penetrating into it, being reflected back from a fish, and passing out into the air again would be reduced to $(0.0012)^2$, or 1.44×10^{-6} of the original sound, during the two trips through the air-water interface. To this great reduction must be added further losses: only a small fraction of the emitted sound would be reflected by a fish, and only a small fraction of what did escape into the air would strike the ears of the listening bat. These figures make it seem almost hopeless for a bat to try to detect fish through the water surface by their echoes, but before dismissing the whole idea as utterly impossible, let us compare what insect-eating bats are known to do in air with the hypothetical location of fish by their echoes.

Certain of the FM bats are able to detect a pebble or a flying insect 1 centimeter in diameter from at least 200 centimeters away. At distances of more than about 10 centimeters from the bat's mouth the sound intensity falls off as the square of the distance. Since a 1-centimeter insect is a small target, sound is scattered from it approximately as it would be from a point source, so that the echo intensity also varies inversely as the square of the distance. Therefore, as the distance from bat to insect increases, the net strength of the echo returning to the animal's ears falls off as the fourth power of the distance. If the insect is twice as far away, the intensity of its echo is $1/2^4$, or 1/16th as great. Let us suppose, for the sake of argument, that a fishing bat does detect a small fish at a distance of 10 centimeters. Since a fish's body is acoustically similar to water, any echo it produces would be most likely to come from the swim bladder. This is an air-filled chamber which most small fresh-water fish have within their bodies, and in a minnow it would be about 1 centimeter, or the same size as the insects detected in air at 200 centimeters. If all other factors were equal, a target at 10 centimeters would return an echo stronger than one at 200 centimeters by a factor of $(200/10)^4$, or 1.6×10^5. The two trips through the water surface would reduce the fish echo by a factor of 1.33×10^{-6}. The product of these two numbers is 0.23, which would mean that the echo received by the fishing bat under these hypothetical conditions would have about one fourth the intensity of the echo which is actually detected by the bat catching insects in air. If this is really a valid comparison, it puts the possibility of catching fish by echoes in quite another light, since a factor of four is well within the uncertainty of the assumptions I have made. For example, the insect-catching bat may well detect 1-centimeter insects at more than 200 centimeters, and an increase in the distance of detection to 280 centimeters would produce an echo from the insect equal to that from the hypothetical fish echo.

This numerical argument, however, does not prove that the fishing bats really do hear echoes from fish through the water surface. It simply means that this possibility merits consideration and should not be rejected out of hand because of the very large energy loss during the two passages through the air-water interface. Or, to put the matter in another way, the detection of insects at 2 meters through the air means that bats are capable of hearing echoes roughly as faint as those that might, under ideal conditions, return from a minnow to a fishing bat. The book *Listening in the Dark* goes into this particular problem in more detail if you wish to pursue it further. But it is significant that a hypothesis which seemed so completely ridiculous when one first learned of the millionfold loss of energy during the round trip from air to water should turn out, on closer examination, to be a serious possibility after all. Common sense and first impressions may be misleading when we are dealing with matters quite outside the range of ordinary human experience upon which people have built what we call common sense.

Resistance to Jamming

Up to this point we have been thinking about echoes as more or less isolated sound waves that could be dealt with one at a time. To be sure, we considered earlier the likelihood that a faint echo would be masked by the louder outgoing sound. Experiments described in Chapter 3 demonstrated that human hearing ignores echoes arriving within a small fraction of a second after a loud sharp click. Bats obviously do better than we in discriminating these echoes from the original sound. In the experiments of Schevill and Lawrence a porpoise showed that it could detect echoes from a small fish despite the louder competing echoes from the bottom of the pond, the surface, and the shore a few feet beyond this small-sized target. But the expertness of bats goes even further than anything we have yet considered. When they are hunting insects, their ears receive a more complicated mixture of sounds than merely their original chirp plus a single echo returning from a single insect and having the same wave form at a lower energy level. What really impinges upon their ears is a whole series of echoes from everything within several feet—the ground, other insects, and every bush, twig, tree trunk, leaf, or blade of grass. Many of these things contribute only small amounts of echo energy, but the echo from an insect is itself a faint one, and if it is audible so must the others be. How then do bats sort out one class of faint echoes from all the others? How do they hear the difference between echoes that mean food to be caught and those that mean obstacles to be dodged?

If we knew how bats discriminate so expertly between faint insect echoes and the competing echoes arriving within a small fraction of a second, we could make more rapid progress toward solving the orientation problems of blind people, to say nothing of developing instruments that could emulate the bats more perfectly. Unfortunately this is not yet possible, but it is interesting to consider how well bats can make such discriminations. This cannot be easy, even for a bat, and faint echoes from wire obstacles are less skillfully utilized when stronger echoes arrive in the same small fraction of a second. For example, we once performed an experiment in which two rows of wires were stretched across a flight room, one row at the middle of the room and the other row 45 centimeters from the end wall, as diagramed in Fig. 12. In both rows the wires extended from floor to ceiling and were spaced 30 centimeters apart. When the diameter of the wires was 0.46 millimeter, they were difficult echo targets, but the percentage of misses in a large number of flights through the central row was 91 per cent. This represents a considerable degree of success, and almost all the contacts were very light touches when the bat did not quite manage to time its wingbeats so that the wing tips cleared the obstacle.

When the same animals not only flew through the middle row but also continued on through the end row, their success was much less—the percentage of misses fell from 91 per cent at the middle row to 58 per cent for the end row which was 45 centimeters from the end wall. This result was probably due to the very much larger echo from the end wall. The situation can be understood in terms of Fig. 14, a schematic graph of the sound energy reaching the bat's ears during the fraction of a second when each chirp is emitted and its several echoes return. The upper graph (A) depicts the situation when the middle row of wires is being detected and avoided; the middle graph (B) applies to the same size of wire located 45 centimeters from the end wall, while the third graph (C) describes a further experiment in which the wires near the end wall were 1.07 millimeters in diameter. In C, the bat's success was about the same (88 per cent misses) as it had been with the 0.46 millimeter wires at the middle of the flight room (A). Under natural conditions the important echoes would be those from an insect rather than a wire, and the competing echoes would arrive from many different objects, such as the ground, tree trunks, or branches of trees. These would produce more complicated echoes than those from the end wall of the flight room and would be present over a longer period of time, but they would never include as strong a single echo as that from the large end wall. An approximation to this case is represented in the fourth graph (D) of Fig. 14, where it has been assumed that some of the extraneous echoes have come from objects closer than the insect itself. This must happen when bats hunt, as they often do,

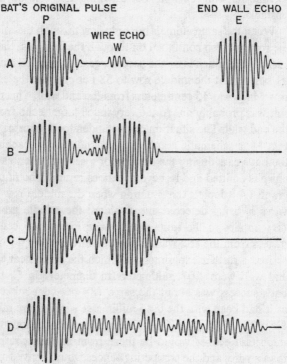

Fig. 14. Schematic graphs of a bat's chirp and the echoes in the flight room (Fig. 12) under various test conditions: A—approaching 0.46-millimeter wires in the middle of room; B—approaching same wires near the end wall; C—approaching larger wires close to the end wall (note the larger echo); and D—approaching an insect under natural conditions in woods where many other objects also return echoes. (For simplicity the frequency modulation is not shown.)

in thickly wooded areas where competing echoes obscure the important echo from the insect.

The success of bats in catching one insect every few seconds testifies to their ability not only to hear the insect echoes but to sort them out of a welter of other, competing echoes. This process has been studied in the laboratory by modifying the circumstances to standardize the conditions and permit measurements of the bats' performance. Rather than studying bats as they hunt insects in the woods, we generated artificial sounds in our flight room so that these noises were added to the echoes from wires, floor, and walls. In other words, we tried to confuse or "jam" the bats. The result was a surprising and revealing failure. The bats continued to dodge wires of 1 to 2 millimeters even in the most intense noise we could produce, a loud hissing that covered the whole frequency range of their orientation sounds. Skillful animals avoided wires of this size just as well in the noise as in the quiet, even though the noise was much louder than the echoes from the wires. These experiments could theoretically be shown as a fifth graph in Fig. 14, but an accurate representation of the noise would obliterate any representation of echoes from the wires.

There are limits, however, to the discriminating ability of even the most skillful bat. If the wires are made smaller and smaller, a size is finally reached where the echoes no longer can be detected. The smallest wire which can be detected in noise is greater than the smallest wire detectable in quiet. For one species of bat the minimum in the quiet was about 0.25 millimeter, and in the noise the minimum size increased to 0.5 to 0.7 millimeter, depending upon the individual animal and its condition at the time of the particular experiment.

(*Listening in the Dark* has a more detailed account of these experiments.)

What emerges from these several examples of orientation based on echoes is the simple fact that bats and porpoises are most adept at locating small and distant objects in this way. Furthermore, they do so with a precision and acuity that are understandable only when one remembers that this is how they make their living. If a bat fumbles with its echoes, it goes hungry. Hunger is a powerful incentive, tending strongly to improve any mechanism or process subjected to this selective action. This is what biologists call *natural selection,* the process responsible for the evolution of plants and animals into their many diversified and complex forms. It is a slow process but an extremely effective one, and in the bats and porpoises we see the end result achieved through natural selection, perfecting over millions of years the animals' faculties for utilizing echoes. Finally, it is important to realize that the use of echoes requires the bats and porpoises to possess more than merely a means for generating sounds that in turn will yield echoes. It is also essential that these animals discriminate certain important echoes from complex mixtures of other sounds that are often much louder than those conveying the crucial information about food.

Discrimination of one portion of a complex sound from louder components is not a special skill of bats and porpoises. All animals endowed with a sense of hearing discriminate, and in many respects the human ear and brain are the best of all. When we listen to speech or music, we sort out a few significant portions of a complicated mixture of shifting wave forms. If we hear people speaking an unknown foreign language, we receive a similar jumble of sound waves, but one to which we have no key. Footsteps or bat chirps and their echoes are a special language of their own. It is much simpler than German, Chinese, or English, but men, particularly blind men, find it very difficult to learn this language. Yet bats no larger than a baby mouse understand it well enough to catch ten mosquitoes every minute in the dark. What is it in a bat's tiny brain that permits understanding of this language and unlocks this library of useful information? No one yet knows the answer. We cannot even be sure we are asking the proper questions.

CHAPTER 5

Sonar and Radar

Although men have not learned the "language of echoes," they have been remarkably successful in designing echolocating instruments which surpass those of animals in many ways but remain quite inferior in other respects. What are these instruments and how do they compare with analogous living mechanisms in the bodies of bats, porpoises, or whirligig beetles? Footsteps and clickers are simple devices that help blind people create more useful echoes, but the receiving instrument is still the human ear. Perhaps blind men will some day learn to exploit the potentialities of the matchless human brain for a better comprehension of the language of echoes. But, in the meantime, it is important to appreciate the devices which men have contrived to carry out both the sending and the receiving functions of echolocation. These mechanisms have been developed for very practical, often military, purposes, excelling particularly in the great distances over which they operate. If they utilize sound waves, they are usually called *sonar* systems. If electromagnetic waves are employed, they are called *radar* systems. Sonar is used by man almost exclusively for underwater echolocation, while radar is used only in air or outer space.

Echoes under Water

The tragic sinking of the *Titanic* by an iceberg in 1912 prompted the first of many efforts to invent a means of detecting icebergs in darkness or in fog. Even in 1959, icebergs caused the sinking of an ocean liner fully equipped with modern aids to navigation. Sir Hiram Maxim, a prolific inventor who in the late nineteenth century attempted to build flying machines, proposed that bats' methods of navigation be copied directly in the design of safety devices for ocean-going ships. Unfortunately, however, he did not really know how bats navigate—for the simple reason that the subject had been largely neglected since the days of Spallanzani. He surmised correctly that bats used echolocation but was incorrect when he assumed that the probing sound came from the beating of their wings. Hence he advised that ships generate very *low*-frequency sounds of roughly 15 c.p.s. and that receiving devices for such frequencies be mounted on the bow of the ship. Faint echoes from this sound were to ring a small bell, loud ones a large gong, so that the crew could judge the seriousness of the danger.

Maxim's idea was, nevertheless, a step forward in understanding bat navigation, for it introduced for the first time the idea that sounds inaudible to human ears might be the basis of bats' uncanny ability to fly in darkness. But his ideas did not lead to any practical method for detecting icebergs, and for at least two important reasons. In the first place, the low frequencies which he proposed meant that long wave lengths would have been involved; 15-c.p.s. sound has a 20-meter wave. It is now well known that objects whose size is much less than the wave length of the sound being used yield only faint echoes, but in 1912 this was not a generally appreciated fact. Had scientists been less scornful of bats and had they known more about "Spallanzani's bat problem," more progress would have been made by 1912. Furthermore, Maxim proposed to echolocate icebergs through the air, whereas both the actual danger to the ship and the major part of the iceberg lay beneath the surface. The latter consideration led other inventors to investigate the possibility of using underwater sound.

Two or three years after the sinking of the *Titanic*, the increasing use of submarines by the German Navy spurred the development of underwater sound devices. At first it was largely a matter of listening to the sounds originating from the submarine, particularly from its engines and propellers. Much of the naval use of underwater sound is still passive listening for the sounds of other ships. But to a small degree by 1918, and to a much greater extent by 1940, research had led to active probing of the sea with sounds which would yield usable echoes. Enemy submarines were the main military targets, but along with the development of sonar came the echo sounder, or fathometer, a device to measure the depth of the water. In comparison with an enemy submarine (or the fish detected by porpoises), the bottom of the ocean would seem to be an easy target, but for many years the idea proved simpler than its realization. In the deeper parts of the ocean even an echo from the bottom was faint and difficult to detect with the early sonar devices, but the most critical problem came when the water was shallower and more dangerous. Here the difficulty was that the ship's hull had a disconcerting tendency to "ring" or prolong the outgoing sound even after the actual generating mechanism had been turned off. The combined sound lasted much longer than the time required for it to make the round trip to the bottom. In other words, there were severe problems of *discrimination*—separating relatively faint echoes from the continuing, original emitted sound. The instruments were confronted with the same problems as those that make a blind man less skilled at echolocation than a porpoise or a bat. This engineering problem was solved in part by learning how to make underwater sounds of shorter duration.

By the 1950s, however, echo sounders had been perfected to a level of reliability where they have become almost essential for safe navigation. They even became so sensitive that they began to indicate "false bottoms" between the ship and the true bottom. "Finding" two or three extra ocean bottoms above the real one was a rather disconcerting discovery, but after a time the fishermen who used echo sounders began to notice that some of the "false bottoms" were really echoes from schools of fish. Still later, mysterious layers of faint echoing, or sound scattering, were noted almost everywhere in deep oceans at several hundred feet below the surface. These have been called the *deep scattering layers* and they were later found to migrate up and down with dawn and dusk. This fact provided the clue to their identity.

Oceanographers had already discovered by systematic netting operations that large populations of shrimp and other small marine animals live at depths where sunlight barely penetrates. This depth is greater at noon than at midnight; hence there is a massive vertical migration of these animals upward during the evening and down again at daybreak. The physical records of the deep scattering layers turned out to match the known behavior of the animals. Once this additional fact was established, the echo sounder became a valuable tool for biological research, for now the timing of the vertical migrations could be studied with great precision. Of course the echoes from a deep scattering layer do not identify the actual animals, so we still do not know for certain whether the principal sources of these echoes are shrimp-like animals, fish, or possibly squid.

Sonar systems effective at echolocating submarines were used with great success in World War II. One of these sonar systems has a transmitting hydrophone, or underwater loudspeaker which broadcasts sound whose power level is 600 watts. For comparison, the minimum sound power level audible in a quiet room at the frequencies to which the human ear is most sensitive is 10^{-16} watt, while a very loud shout at close range has a power of 10^{-4} watt. Thus this sonar system puts into the ocean a sound power roughly equivalent to that of 6,000,000 loud shouts. These intense probing sounds are emitted as short pulses lasting one or two tenths of a second. The frequency can be set anywhere between 10,000 and 26,000 c.p.s. Since the velocity of sound in sea water is about 1500 meters/second, the actual wave lengths of these sounds are from 5 to 13 centimeters, and the length of the pulse is from 150 to 300 meters.

Because this system emits some frequencies above the range of human hearing, there has to be a system to make these frequencies audible. You may be familiar with the "beat note," or "beat frequency" which is conspicuous when two nearly identical notes are sounded simultaneously. If one note is 500 c.p.s. and the other is 600 c.p.s., you will hear a third note of 100 c.p.s. Hence in the electrical circuit of the sonar apparatus, by generating a local frequency and combining with it the incoming echo, an audible beat note is generated. For instance, an incoming echo of 22,000 c.p.s. and a local frequency of 23,000 c.p.s. produce an audible note of 1000 c.p.s. Since the emitted sounds were of short duration, the beat note was also short and sounded like "ping." So familiar was this noise to antisubmarine sailors that probing with sound came to be called "pinging."

In selecting the frequencies of the underwater sound which will produce the most useful echoes, the same general considerations apply as apply to echolocation by bats or blind men. Short pulses are desirable because they allow the emitted sound to end before the echo returns. This means that the frequency of the waves within the pulse cannot be too low; otherwise the pulse duration allows time for only one or two sound waves. Even submarines are small enough targets that long wave lengths could become inefficient owing to the smaller echo returned by an object smaller than one wave length. Furthermore, the background noise always present in the sea is greater at lower frequencies. On the other hand, in water as in air, there is an increasing loss of sound energy as the frequency increases because of the absorption of sound as it travels through the water. Bats have evolved a most satisfactory machinery for echolocation, but men designing sonar systems had to balance all these factors against one another in reaching the compromise choice of 10,000–26,000 c.p.s. as a useful range for practical echo ranging.

In view of the fact that many of the most successful bats use signals with a rapid frequency change during each brief pulse of sound, it is interesting to find that sonar engineers developed a somewhat similar procedure which sometimes improves the performance of the system. In one type of operation the frequency of the emitted sonar signal was varied continuously from 800 c.p.s. above to 800 cycles below the regular frequency. This change was made to occur, as it does in the pulses of the FM bats, during each individual pulse of sound. When the echoes of such pulses were received, the frequency change was audible in the beat note. In one typical setting of the apparatus the transmitted frequency, and of course the echo, was varied from 20,800 to 19,200 c.p.s. If the local frequency was set at 19,000 c.p.s., the beat note would vary from 1800 to 200 c.p.s. and this would produce an extreme chirp or "Wheeoough" sound. One advantage of this type of operation was that at any particular instant of time the many reverberations or multiple echoes from the ship's hull and the water surface had traveled different distances and hence had different frequencies as they arrived at the receiving hydrophone. This tended to create an audible difference between the important chirping echoes from a submarine and the noise level of reverberation from which they had to be discriminated. The important echo was a clear chirp, the competing reverberations an irregular and shifting mixture of frequencies. Very likely bats obtain a similar advantage from their frequency-modulated pulses.

In another type of operation the sonar system used a constant frequency in the emitted pulse, and the operator listened for slight differences in the pitch of the audible beat note. Slight differences between the echo frequency and the local frequency can produce large changes in the audible ping. These differences can be used to determine the relative motion of the target by means of what is called the *Doppler effect*. This change in frequency resulting from the motion of the source causes the rising pitch of a train whistle as the train approaches you. To understand the Doppler effect, let us consider a concrete example. Suppose that the sonar ship is moving east at 10 meters per second while emitting a 0.1 second pulse of 20,000 c.p.s. sound, that is,

2000 sound waves altogether. Let us simplify our arithmetic by assuming that the velocity of sound in sea water is exactly 1500 meters per second. If the ship were stationary, the pulse would occupy 1500 × 0.1, or 150 meters of distance through the water. But it is moving at 10 meters per second, or 1 meter in the one tenth second required to emit the 2000-wave pulse. Since the transmitting hydrophone pursued the sound waves and covered 1 meter while emitting the pulse, the train of waves was thereby compressed into 149 meters instead of 150. This does not affect the velocity of sound in sea water, so that a passing porpoise would hear the pulse as 2000 waves occupying 149 meters and traveling like all other sound waves at 1500 meters per second. All the waves of the pulse strike the porpoise in 140/1500, or 0.099 second, and their frequency would therefore be 2000 waves in 0.099 second, or 20,202 c.p.s. In other words, the emitted pulse has a higher frequency to the listening porpoise because the ship has moved during the process of emitting it. The velocity of sound depends entirely upon the medium in which it is traveling, not upon the velocity of the sound source.

Let us carry our example a little further and suppose that this pulse strikes a submarine which is moving west, toward the sonar ship, also at 10 meters per second. The pulse, which was 149 meters long as it passed the porpoise, is further compressed during the 0.1 second while it is colliding with the oncoming submarine. As it is bouncing back from the target, it is again compressed, both times by the same factor of 149/150. It is not necessarily easy to see why this compression occurs *twice* on striking the submarine, but an imaginary modification of the physical events may help. Suppose that the submarine did not return the echo by immediate reflection but rather was equipped with a hydrophone and tape recorder so that the pulse was stored on tape. Suppose that at some later time this recording was played back into the water. The compression would occur during both reception and rebroadcast of the sound waves, since in both cases the submarine would be moving relative to the water. Now suppose that the delay between recording and playback is made less and less. Nothing we do while shortening the delay time would affect the compression of the train of sound waves, so that there will still be *two* such compressions regardless of whether the delay is long or short. If the delay is very short, it approaches zero, and zero delay brings us back to the original situation of immediate reflection. Thus the porpoise hears the echo as 2000 waves occupying only about 147 meters. To be sure, one can split hairs and say that $150 \times 149/150 \times 149/150 \times 149/150$ are a very little more than 147. But it is not much more, and I promised to keep our arithmetic as simple as possible.

Finally the 2000 sound waves reach the receiving hydrophone of the sonar ship, which is still advancing at 10 meters per second to meet them, and the same compression is repeated for the last time. The end result is that the receiving circuit of the sonar system gets the 2000 waves in a shorter time than was required to send them out. The amount of this shortening is $0.1 - 0.1 \left(\frac{149}{150} \right)^4$, or approximately 0.03 second.

The Doppler effect can be somewhat simplified by considering only the relative motion of the sonar system and its target; in this example the two were approaching at 20 meters per second. The pulse length of the received echo is then reduced by the square of the ratio of the relative velocity of approach to the velocity of sound. It is obvious that if the two ships were moving away from each other, the Doppler effect would work in the opposite direction, and the net effect would be a reduction in the frequency of the echo.

To return to our specific example, the final echo has a frequency at the sonar ship of $20,000 \times (\frac{150}{149})^4$, or about 20,540 c.p.s. If this is translated into an audible ping by combining it with a local frequency of 19,000 c.p.s., the echo beat note will be 1540 c.p.s., whereas if both ships were stationary, the beat note would be 1000 c.p.s. This is a fairly extreme example of rapid approach of the two ships, but in actual practice sonar operators can tell when a submarine turns or even when it speeds up or slows down. Though we understand far less of what goes on in a bat or porpoise brain than we know about the operation of this sonar system, it is reasonable to infer that similar comparisons of outgoing and echo frequencies may well be used to detect the motion of flying insects or swimming fish. The horseshoe bats with their constant frequency pulses can perhaps make better use of the Doppler effect than can the FM bats, but even the latter seem to use less frequency sweep when closing on insect prey than during cruising flights when they are presumably seeking to make their initial contact and detection.

Prospecting by Echo

Sound waves are not limited to air and water; they can also travel through solid materials of any kind. Even the echo sounder designed only to echolocate the bottom may sometimes show a type of false bottom different from the fish echoes or deep scattering layer described earlier. Sometimes the records indicate a second or third bottom *below* the real one rather than above it. This means that after the bottom echo of the probing pulse has returned to the ship's hull a further echo returns somewhat later. On first seeing such a record, an experienced physicist might surmise that the pulse had made two round trips through the depth of water under the ship's hull—down to the bottom, up to the surface, down to the bottom again, and finally back as a second echo. This can indeed happen, but then the time of arrival of the second echo is almost exactly twice that required by the first. Many of the false bottoms that seem to lie below the real bottom result from echoes returning at other times than twice the travel time of the first, direct echo. What really happens under certain conditions is that some of the sound energy penetrates into the mud or sand of the ocean floor, travels downward through it, and is then reflected back again by some sudden discontinuity such as a layer of rock of different hardness or density. Making due allowances for the velocity of sound transmission through the material just below the bottom of the ocean, geologists can estimate rather accurately the depth below the bottom at which this discontinuity occurs. Without even intending to do so, designers and users of echo sounders have thus hit upon a method of echolocation underground.

Quite purposefully and for many years, other geologists have been studying the transmission of sound waves through miles of the earth's crust. Earthquakes produce vibrations that can be detected by delicate vibration detectors known as seismographs. So do man-made explosions if they are sufficiently violent. Blasting in mines and quarries can be detected miles away, and the seismographic detection of nuclear explosions has now become a matter of major importance, a hotly debated issue at international conferences. By comparing the vibration records resulting from earthquakes at different points around the world, it is possible to deduce that some waves travel close to the surface, others through deeper layers of rock, while still others travel hundreds of miles below the surface. Careful study of the times of arrival of such waves at different listening stations has enabled geologists to learn much more than they could have determined by any other method about the composition of our planet. (The Science Study book *How Old Is the Earth* goes into this subject in more detail.)

The actual waves recorded by a seismograph are of quite low frequency, and they are usually so irregular that it is difficult or even meaningless to describe them in terms of frequencies. Major components vary from about 0.5 to 5 c.p.s. They also differ from sound waves in air or water in that they involve motion in directions other than the direction of wave propagation. There are several different types of seismic waves, classified according to the relative degrees of motion in various directions. By painstaking analysis of recordings made at various points above and below the ground and in different directions from the place of a test explosion, geologists can locate many kinds of rock structures below the surface. This procedure has been of great use in prospecting for oil, or rather for the types of rock and salt deposits that are commonly associated with it. Much of our industrial economy has been made possible by the success of this method for echolocating oil.

Echoes versus X-rays

Sound waves have also come into widespread use for harmless testing of materials such as metals and rubber. If the material is pure and homogeneous, it transmits sound waves in a smooth and orderly way. But if there are discontinuities, such as air bubbles in castings or

118

defects in tire casings, they distort transmitted sound waves. In some cases very short pulses of sound are used to produce distinct echoes in the material being tested. The sound frequencies are often very high, up to 1 megacycle per second (10^6 c.p.s.), and this is possible because relatively short distances of transmission are involved. It is a comparatively inexpensive method of testing compared to structural failure of an important and costly machine, and the material is not damaged in any way.

Recently this sort of acoustic probing has been applied to the living bodies of animals and men. It is possible to detect discontinuities in our internal organs in this way, using sound waves generated at the surface of the body by suitable sound sources, such as crystals which are vibrated at high frequencies by electric currents. This method is not without its dangers, for intense sound waves in our bodies can produce damage. But, when properly controlled, the method has some advantages over X-rays. At least any damage is local and, insofar as we know, is not a long-delayed effect on our genes—the complex molecules in our reproductive organs, some of which may in time determine what our children will be like. One limitation of this method stems from the large number of discontinuities that are naturally present in a human body—those between muscle and bone, digestive tract and blood vessels, heart and lungs, etc. Thus any abnormalities must be discriminated from a complex background of natural structures, and this makes it more difficult to locate a tumor in a human brain than an air bubble in a cast-iron pipe. Nevertheless, this new means for studying our invisible insides may lead in time to safer or more effective methods of locating internal disorders in an early and curable stage. The discrimination problems may be no more difficult than those facing a blind man or a bat, and human ingenuity may eventually solve this type of problem along with the others mentioned in previous chapters.

Radar

The detection of distant aircraft by echoes of radio waves stands as one of mankind's major technical accomplishments. In military results alone it has well repaid the billions of dollars spent on its development and on manufacture of military radar systems. Not only can ground- or ship-based radar systems detect airplanes at hundreds of miles but smaller radars carried on airplanes can locate other aircraft and also resolve a surprising amount of detail on the ground below. Radar systems developed for the purpose can draw crude but highly useful maps of hundreds of square miles of terrain in a fraction of a second. The maps are drawn on specialized cathode-ray oscilloscope screens. Radar echoes can also be used to locate and track clouds and storms, birds and locusts, meteors, earth satellites, and ballistic missiles. Shortly after World War II, radar echoes were successfully detected from the moon. In 1958, for the first time, very faint echoes from the planet Venus were detected. Although this book cannot discuss radar thoroughly, certain basic similarities are well worth considering, and it is even possible to make a rough comparison of the performance and efficiencies of radar systems and natural living systems that have evolved to enable bats to navigate and catch insects in the dark.

Relative Efficiency of Bats and Radar

As with the sonar system we discussed, this comparison will be based on radar systems that served well in

World War II and have since been retired to pasture—replaced by somewhat more efficient models. To make the comparison more meaningful, I have selected a typical airborne radar set which was a real triumph of engineering skill in that it accomplished, with a relatively small weight and power consumption, as much as many previous models that were far bulkier and less efficient. This radar operated at a frequency of 9375 megacycles $(\lambda = 3 \times \dfrac{10^{10}}{9.375} \times 10^9)$, or a wave length of 3.2 centimeters. While this frequency is vastly higher than those used by bats, porpoises, or naval sonar systems, the wave length is not greatly different because of the much higher velocity of light or other electromagnetic radiation. Where our sonar system emitted its acoustic signals at a peak power level of 600 watts, this radar developed a peak power of 10,000 watts. It is important to stress that none of these systems, living or instrumental, emits power continuously; all have a relatively low duty cycle, or ratio of time on to time off. In typical operation this radar emitted pulses lasting 0.8 microsecond $(8 \times 10^{-7}$ second) at a pulse repetition rate of 810 pulses per second. In other words, every 1/810th second, or 1.23×10^{-3} second it emitted a pulse lasting 8×10^{-7} second, followed by a silent interval about 1500 times as long. This left ample time for echoes to return (at the velocity of light) before the next pulse arrived. The entire radar system weighed 124 pounds, but this does not include the weight of the airplane generator which supplied the electric power. This radar set detected aircraft at 50 miles under most conditions and was a brilliant operational success. It is therefore of some interest to inquire how well it compares with bat systems, watt for watt of power emitted and gram for gram of weight.

This comparison is not a simple one because of the

widely different circumstances in which the two classes of echo-ranging systems are actually used. Bats are interested in detecting small insects at a few feet or yards. The user of an airborne radar wishes to locate objects on the ground and other airplanes some miles away. Bats use sound waves, while radar employs radio waves of only slightly greater wave lengths. Bats maneuver very rapidly, the whole sequence of detection, turning toward an insect, intercepting, catching, and swallowing, all occurring within 1 second. In ordinary use of an airborne radar, the operator sees a spot on his oscilloscope screen, notes how it changes in position relative to his own flight path, and then takes appropriate action. This may vary all the way from a turn to avoid any danger of collision, if the two airplanes are airliners, to a close pursuit and firing of a machine gun or rocket at the other plane if it is an enemy in time of war. In both cases the whole operation may be accomplished by a man sitting in a darkened cabin looking only at spots on his radar screen. The bat does it all within one second, in the dark, with a brain smaller than the eraser on a pencil.

To make comparison a quantitative one, we can best tabulate the important quantities which are known for the two systems and on which we may base estimates of their relative efficiencies. The table on page 123 gives approximately the range of the radar and also its weight and power requirements. An efficient system for echo-location should detect the smallest possible objects at the greatest possible distances and it should do so with the least possible power and the lightest possible apparatus. Bulky installations of whirling machinery may be impressive at first glance, but unnecessary complexity and power expenditure are actually signs of inefficiency. With this in mind, let us set up an efficiency index, an equation which will evaluate the combination of these four important factors. Such an index should have a high value for the most efficient systems and should be roughly proportional to the relative efficiencies of the various systems of echolocation that we compare. As will become clear a little later, this is not as simple as it might seem, but the process of attempting to define such an index, and then modifying it as may seem necessary, will in itself prove to be helpful in calling attention to the various quantitative considerations that are important for echolocation.

TABULAR COMPARISONS OF BATS AND RADAR

	AN/APS − 10 radar system	Big brown bat	Little brown bat
Target detected	Airplane	Insect	Wire
Target diameter, d (cm)	300	1	1.8×10^{-2}
Range of detection, R (cm)	8×10^6	200	90
Weight of apparatus, W (grams)	9×10^4	0.1	0.05
Emitted power, P (watts)	10^4	10^{-5}	10^{-6}
R/PWd	2.9×10^{-5}	2×10^8	10^{11}
R^4/PWd^2	5×10^{13}	1.6×10^{15}	3.8×10^{17}
R^4/PWd^4	5.5×10^8	1.6×10^{15}	1.2×10^{22}

The above table lists the range of detection, R, the diameter of the target, d, (both in centimeters), the power emission, P (watts), and the weight of the system, W (grams). For the bats, 10 per cent of the weight of a fasting animal seems a generous allowance for the larynx, ears, auditory portions of the brain, and the other parts used directly for echolocation. For both bat and radar the power is the peak level reached during each pulse. It may be recalled from Chapter 2 that the ears of bats and men operate at sound power levels ranging from about 10^{-16} to 10^{-4} watt per square centimeter. The airborne radar detection of another airplane at 50 miles is compared with two cases of echolocation by bats—the detection of a 1-centimeter insect (or pebble) by a big brown bat at 2 meters, and the echolocation of a 0.18-millimeter wire by a little brown bat at 90 centimeters.

The first approach to defining the efficiency index might be simply to have R, the distance of detection, in the numerator, and the other three quantities, P (power), W (weight), and d (target size), in the denominator, where large values will tend to lower the index. This index, R/PWd, is listed in the next row of the table, and when judged on this basis, the bats appear billions of times better than the radar system. But a little reflection shows that, in defining the index in this way, we have made an important assumption; namely, that these four quantities are really related to one another as we have entered them in the equation. For example, this definition of efficiency assumes that range will increase in direct proportion to power. But for all radar systems, and probably all bats, the emitted energy falls off as the square of the distance. And most small targets send back echoes that also obey the inverse-square law. As pointed out in Chapter 4, where insect-catching bats were compared with the hypothetical case of a bat attempting to echolocate fish through the air-water interface, the energy in an echo is proportional to $1/R^4$. This means that to obtain twice the range a system of echolocation will need 2^4, or 16 times as much power, and we should therefore change our index to contain R to the fourth power instead of the first. This will greatly increase the rating scored by the radar set detecting an airplane at 50 miles.

Having made this improvement in the index, we should also scrutinize the other variables in our equation, in particular the size of the target, d. If a series of targets is fairly large relative to the wave length of the signal being used to generate an echo, the echo power is usually proportional roughly to their areas, or to d^2. This is true of most radar targets, and certainly of airplanes being echolocated with 3.2-centimeter waves. Is it also true for bats? The insects they catch vary from somewhat below one wave length to several wave lengths, and of course the FM bats employ orientation sounds containing a whole octave of frequencies, or a twofold range of wave lengths in each pulse. It is probably reasonable to assume that in insect detection the echo power varies as the square of the target diameter, although in some cases the insects may be enough below one wave length so that this assumption would lead to an overestimate of the echo strength. The next line of the table therefore lists for each of the three systems the value of the revised efficiency index, R^4/PWd^2. Even on this basis the bats are somewhat superior to the radar.

Finally, we should pay a little more attention to the bats which detect wires far smaller than one wave length, such as the little brown bat listed in the third row of the table. When wires or other cylindrical obstacles are much smaller than one wave length, the echo power varies as d^4, and the 0.18-millimeter wires detected at 90 centimeters are certainly in this size range. This domain of target size produces what is sometimes called *Rayleigh scattering,* after the nineteenth-century physicist who analyzed it with special reference to light scattered by tiny particles in the air. Such light makes up most of what we see in the sky, and since the particles are of less than the wave lengths of visible light (4 to 7×10^{-5} centimeter), short wave length light is more strongly scattered than other colors. This is why the sky is blue. By analogy we might say that the bat flying up to these wires must hear "blue echoes." In any event, a case could be made for evaluating bat sonar by means of an index containing d^4 rather than d or d^2, and the value of R^4/PWd^4 is therefore listed in the last line of the table.

The drastic results of changing the definition of our efficiency index should now be clear. This may indeed open serious questions as to whether such different systems for echolocation can be meaningfully compared on a simple numerical basis. Furthermore, several other important factors have not yet been brought into the comparison. Bats operating with sound waves in air face serious reductions in echo signal due to the absorption of sound in air, especially at higher frequencies. During the round trip from bat to target and return, sound of 50 kc loses power by a factor of 0.63 for every meter of distance, in addition to the reduction due to the inverse fourth power reduction for echoes. At 100 kc the reduction is by a factor of 0.44 over every meter. Radio waves suffer no such severe losses in traveling through the air. This fact puts the bat at a great disadvantage over long distances. On the other hand, there is a consideration which would favor most radar systems as compared to bats. This is the duty cycle, or fraction of the time during which energy is being emitted. In typical cases, such as those included in our table, a bat would be emitting 10 to 20 pulses per second, each pulse lasting 2 to 5 milliseconds, so that the duty cycle would vary between 0.02 and 0.1. The radar had a far lower duty cycle, however, the interval between pulses having been about 1500 times as long as the pulse itself, so that the duty cycle would be about 0.0007. This means that if we were to use average power rather than peak power in our comparison, the bats would suffer by a factor of about 100. Yet a partisan of the bats might offer in rebuttal the consideration that we allowed 10 per cent of the animal's weight for its sonar apparatus, whereas the weight of the radar set was a much smaller fraction of the mass of the airplane that carried it. From the bat's point of view it would perhaps be more valid to compare its whole weight with that of the entire airplane.

If we take the broadest view, it is obvious that bats and other living animals are vastly more efficient than radars and airplanes, even though it is difficult to attach numbers to the comparison. Bats maintain and repair their living machinery; airplanes and radar sets must be manufactured and repaired by men. Bats catch and digest all the food that provides power for their bodily mechanisms; airplanes are not expected to refuel by catching birds, and the fuel pumped to them requires no chemical processing in the plane before use. Nor do any artifical mechanisms reproduce themselves. The unusual aspect of the comparison we have been making is that a living mechanism can be compared directly with a radar set on almost the same terms that an engineer would employ in comparing one radar with another. The results of the comparison inspire a healthy respect for the mechanisms of flesh and blood which have evolved in nature under the pressure of natural selection.

CHAPTER 6

Suppose You Were Blind

In the preceding chapters we have examined waves and echoes to understand better how animals and men have used them to locate objects which are essential for survival. Such studies of natural phenomena often seem useless to all but a very few people, but so do many scientific explorations. Yet history has clearly shown that men have improved their lot by investigations into the unknown. However insignificant it may have seemed at the time, there is a true inner satisfaction in discovering new relationships and new information to add to our understanding of the world around us. We often hope that observations and new facts can one day be used to improve our environment still further. What could be more beneficial than trying to apply this new-found knowledge to men who cannot see with their eyes? Can we help them to "see" with their ears—to learn the language of echoes?

Blindness is always a tragedy for human beings because our brains and our whole way of life are built around light and vision. But men's eyes are not their only channels of communication with the rest of the world, and sound is in some ways even more useful. For example, we can see somewhat less than 1 octave of frequencies, or wave lengths, roughly from 4 to 7.5×10^{-7} centimeter. Our sense of hearing, on the other hand, extends from about 20 to 20,000 c.p.s., a range of a thousandfold, or approximately 10 octaves. Audible sound can thus contain a much richer variety of frequencies than visible light, and this is partly why sound rather than light is used for speech. Of course, there are other reasons; for instance, living organisms cannot generate light, except for a few luminescent animals and plants.

The sharp shadows cast by light make it less useful as a vehicle for speech and short-range communication. Just because sound does go around corners, it is useful in calling and signaling, particularly when almost every motion and contact between a person or animal and the physical world around it generates some sound. The great advantage of light to us is that it has short wave lengths and, consequently, objects of small size give off specular reflections. It is for this reason that eyes and lenses can focus sharp images. Only when one tries to use a microscope to see objects about the size of the wave length of light does that wave length become an important limitation. An object must be smaller than one micron (one millionth of a meter) before it scatters light rather than reflecting it.

If sound waves and light waves did not already exist, we well might find scientists trying to invent them, one to form sharp images and permit accurate observations of small details, the other with a wide-frequency spectrum to convey complex information with a minimum of interference from shadow-casting obstacles. The two types complement each other, and while the loss of our sense organs for either is a major handicap, there is enough duplication of what each can do to permit some substitution of one after losing the other.

The Sense of Obstacles

Blindness has been an all-too-common affliction of men, and while no device or procedure can completely replace lost sight, blind men for centuries have learned to get about in the world and carry on a surprising number of activities. Some become so skillful at avoiding obstacles and maintaining an adequate general orientation that it is difficult for a stranger to realize they are really blind. For example, there was once a blind boy who learned when six years old to ride his tricycle all about the sidewalks near his home without injury or accident. When he approached pedestrians, he steered around them, and he always knew when to turn corners without going into the street. Other blind people travel widely in busy cities, crossing streets, using buses and trains, dodging lampposts and wire fences. How do they detect these obstacles before touching them? Many theories have been advanced, both by the blind people themselves and by those who have worked or lived with them. Curiously enough, the most skillful of the blind differ widely in their explanations of their own abilities. Many say they feel with their hands or faces the proximity of obstacles, and the term "facial vision" has come into wide use to describe their orientation to objects which are too far away to feel or touch. Others believe that hearing is somehow involved; still others speak of "pressures" and other ill-defined sensations that warn them of dangers just ahead.

The central question is obviously the nature of the physical message that travels from the obstacles to the blind man, and the way in which his remaining sense organs detect and interpret this information from the outside world. From about 1890 to 1940 many studies were made of the "sense of obstacles," but only in the early 1940s was a conclusive answer obtained from carefully controlled experiments. While these experiments were performed by men who called themselves psychologists, the experiments can be considered classic examples of *biophysics,* the application to problems posed by living organisms of the same basic principles of investigation that have developed physics as a rigorous science. The chief difference between biophysics, thus broadly defined, and the physics of non-living systems is the greater degree of complexity and refinement of living organisms. Animals and men are made of far more intricate mechanisms than clickers and ripple tanks, microscopes or television sets, and this is why our understanding of biological processes is so much less thorough and complete than our knowledge of physics or chemistry.

The psychologists, or biophysicists, who finally solved the question of obstacle perception by the blind were Professor Karl M. Dallenbach of Cornell University, and two graduate students, one of whom, Michael Supa, was himself totally blind. Milton Cotzin, the other student, had normal vision, but he and others who served as experimental subjects wore blindfolds for many hours at a time in order to experience what life is like for the blind, and, in particular, to develop as much as possible the ability to detect obstacles before bumping into them. First the experimenters set up a sort of obstacle course, a long hallway down which the subject walked and across which was placed a large screen of fiberboard at some point chosen by the experimenter. This location was varied from trial to trial, so that the subject never knew whether it was 6, 10, 18, 24, or 30 feet ahead of the starting point, or even whether it was there at all. His task was to walk along the hallway, say when he first thought he was approaching the screen, and then walk up as close as he could without striking it.

Some of the subjects, both blind and blindfolded, could judge accurately the presence or absence of the screen at several feet and then move in until their faces were within a few inches before deciding that any further approach would bring them into contact with it. The phenomenon of obstacle detection was thus brought into the laboratory in a manner which allowed it to be studied repeatedly under reasonably constant conditions. This step is often a crucial one in attacking scientific problems of this sort. Elusive and unpredictable events are very much more difficult to study than those which can be repeated under known conditions. Only in the latter case is it fairly easy to vary the factors that seem likely to be important and then observe the results. Earlier studies of obstacle detection by the blind had been plagued with great variability in the performance of the subjects. That mainly is why they had not led to clear and decisive answers. Yet Supa, Cotzin, and Dallenbach built their experimental design on the extensive, if inconclusive, experience of earlier experimenters. Without this background they would probably not have been able to devise such decisive experiments.

Once they had arranged conditions where blind or blindfolded people were regularly detecting a standardized test obstacle, the next step was the theoretically obvious but nevertheless rather difficult one of eliminating one possible channel of sensory communication at a time, while leaving the subject with free use of the others. One leading theory was that the skin supplied some kind of sensation of touch or pressure when obstacles were nearby; another was that sound played a major role. The practical problem in testing the "skin pressure theory" was to shield the subjects' skin from any possible influence that might be arriving from the obstacle, and this was doubly difficult because no one could say what this might be—air currents, electromagnetic radiation, heat or cold, or possibly some sort of energy not known to physics. To test the sound theory, the logical procedure was to prevent sounds from reaching the subjects' ears without interfering with whatever the skin might be feeling as a result of proximity to the obstacles. The covering of the skin clearly had to be accomplished without interfering with the subjects' hearing, and vice versa. The final outfit that the subjects were obliged to wear consisted of a long veil of thick felt which covered the head and shoulders, plus heavy leather gloves to shield the hands. Ordinary clothing covered the rest of the body surface. Such was the protection that they could not feel even the air current of an electric fan directed at their heads. After some preliminary trials to accustom them to walking about in this "armor," the subjects found they could detect the screen almost as well as ever. The average distance of first detection had been 6.9 feet with no veil or gloves, and it was now reduced only slightly —to 5.25 feet. This seemed to dispose of the possibility that obstacles were detected by feeling them through the skin, despite the fact that originally some of this group of subjects, like many blind people, were certain that they *felt* the obstacles with the hands or face.

The next experiment was to leave the hands and face completely free but to cover the subjects' ears. Earlier experiments of this kind had given conflicting results; sometimes the detection of obstacles was impaired, sometimes not. Complete exclusion of sound by earplugs is not possible, but Supa, Cotzin, and Dallenbach wished to be sure that as little sound as possible reached their subjects. They therefore wore earplugs of wax and cotton, ear muffs, and padding over the sides of the head. This compound series of barriers was necessary because many sounds, particularly those of low frequency, penetrate ordinary earplugs or ear muffs. Everyone knows from the ordinary experience of wearing ear muffs or parka hoods in cold weather that by speaking slightly louder than usual one can still converse with his companions no matter how well the ears are protected from the winter winds.

So thorough was this muffling that the subjects could not hear the sounds of their own footsteps, and instructions could only be given them by loud shouts. A loud shout can easily have 10^9 times the energy of a barely audible whisper. Direct measurement of the intensity necessary for them to detect a test sound showed that their auditory sensitivity had been reduced by a factor of about 4,000,000; that is, they could hear the test sound only after its energy level had been increased four millionfold above the level that was just audible without the ear covering.

When the same subjects were now asked to repeat the experiments with their hearing thus impaired, the results were spectacular. None retained any obstacle-detection ability at all, and in each of one hundred trials every subject bumped unexpectedly into the screen. One of the blind men, who had stoutly maintained that sound played no part at all in his "facial vision," complained that he was now getting no sensation at all, and for the first time he walked hesitantly and held out his hands to guard against anticipated accidents. If sound does account for the obstacle-detection ability, one might ask why there was any reduction in distance of first detection when the subjects wore the felt veil and leather gloves.

This was probably due to the reduction in sound level caused by the shielding effect of the bulky hood.

Guiding Echoes

These experiments would seem to have settled the matter once and for all, but criticisms would still have been possible if the experimenters had stopped at this point. Perhaps the pressure of the ear covering was disturbing some subtle tactile sense. Perhaps blind men were warned of obstacles not by hearing as such but by some special kind of pressure sense involving the ear canal or adjacent areas of skin. Even men who had studied this subject for years were skeptical that sound waves could be the messengers by which blind people detected obstacles. Further, many blind men themselves still continued to think they *felt* obstacles. To convince such skeptics it was necessary to modify the experiment so that sound and only sound carried the necessary information from the outside world into the subject's nervous system. This might seem a hopeless task; if the experiments described above were unconvincing, what arguments could hope to overcome such skepticism?

The answer was to employ a telephone system to transmit the appropriate sounds to the subject sitting in a remote and soundproof room. The sounds transmitted over the telephone wires were those picked up by a microphone carried by a man walking along the same obstacle course. They were similar, though not identical, to what the man would hear himself if he were listening for evidence that the screen was just ahead.

The results of the telephone experiment were astonishingly close to those obtained by the same subjects in the original tests. They could sit in the soundproof room and decide by listening to the telephone whether the screen was being approached or not. After some practice they could detect the screen at an average distance of 6.4 feet, only a little less than their average of 6.9 feet when they were doing their own walking and listening. Such a result would seem to dispel all doubts; surely no one could argue now that anything but sound was involved. But scientists who have studied problems like this have learned to be extremely cautious. Many experiments which have seemed this convincing have turned out to be misleading. Suppose, for example, that the person who walked up to the screen with the microphone changed his breathing rhythm or the sounds of his footsteps and thus unconsciously conveyed to the remote listener his proximity to the screen? This sort of unconscious signaling has been known to occur, and, incidentally, it accounts for many cases of what has been interpreted as mental telepathy.

This worry led to further experiments in which the second person was replaced by a motor-driven cart which carried the microphone towards the screen. The subject in the soundproof room controlled the movements of the cart while listening to the sounds the microphone picked up. As often happens in a scientific experiment, new facts raise new questions—one often ends up with more questions than he had at the beginning. Here the question raised was of major importance. Granted that sounds could be conveyed over the telephone system, what were the actual sounds that told the listener the screen was near? In the original experiment no special effort was made to generate sounds or produce echoes; indeed, the experimenters in the beginning had been uncertain that sounds were really of any consequence. They had simply tried to bring phenomenon into the laboratory and arrange conditions under which it could be repeatedly studied. But having learned that sound, rather than anything which could not travel along telephone wires, informed the blind man that the screen was in front of him, the experimenters had to consider the nature of these sounds.

Footsteps were an obvious possibility, and when the original experiments were repeated with the subjects walking in their stocking feet on a soft carpet, their ability to detect the screen was greatly reduced. The average distance of first detection fell from 6.9 feet when the subjects were wearing shoes and walking on the bare floor to 3.4 feet when the sounds of their footsteps were dampened by the carpet. Some subjects snapped their fingers or made clucking sounds, but others apparently relied on whatever sounds were present in the hallway, such as the sound of their own breathing or the rustle of their clothing. This question had not been seriously considered in the design of the first experiments, but now that the investigation had reached the point where the microphone was to be mounted on a cart there would be no sound from footsteps or breathing. Some other sound had to be substituted, which provided the opportunity to study the usefulness of various sounds in providing audible clues to the presence or absence of obstacles. Obviously, too, the experiment involved echoes. If some sound told a listener that the screen was present, it must have been a sound which was different with the screen than without it.

In order to study the character of the echoes used by blind people, the experimenters then equipped the cart with a loudspeaker as well as a microphone. A variety of sounds with known characteristics could now be generated by the loudspeaker for further tests. If a loud hissing noise was used—that is, a noise containing a wide range of audible frequencies—the screen could be detected by the subjects listening to the telephone in the

soundproof room. The distance of first detection aver-
aged 3.75 feet, less than the range of detection when in
an earlier test a person carried the microphone toward
the screen. Nevertheless, it was an impressive performance, considering how greatly the situation had been al-
tered from the first series of experiments. Other sounds
were also tried, but the experiments were concluded before the ideal sound had been discovered which men
might use to obtain the more revealing echoes. The investigations ended because the original problem had
been conclusively solved by the proof that sounds and,
in particular, echoes were the messages that inform blind
men about the existence and position of obstacles.

One significant feature of this important discovery is
the striking divergence between the subjective feelings of
many blind people and all the objective evidence which
we have examined. When a man has developed the remarkable ability to find his way about through the bus-
tling traffic of a modern city in what to him is total
darkness, and when he does this so skillfully and un-
obtrusively that one can travel with him for hours and
never suspect that he is blind, then it is natural to assume
that he knows what he is doing and how he does it. But
often the expert blind man can say only that he somehow "feels" his way and "knows" before he bumps into
the tree or fence post that it is there. If questioned more
closely, he may say he feels the proximity of the object
with his hands, his face, or his forehead. Yet when the
process of obstacle detection is studied under controlled
conditions, it is clear that sounds and hearing are the
essential ingredients. In addition, the whole surface of
the blind man's skin can be covered by heavy felt or
leather without preventing him from detecting obstacles
before he strikes them. When his ears are plugged, he
no longer "feels" the obstacles with his hands or face,

and if he continues on his way, he invariably strikes them without warning. Subjective impressions obviously can be misleading—we do not always know just which of our senses is informing us about our surroundings. This is not to say that our senses are not keen, but rather that our conscious thinking about them may lead us to the wrong conclusion about how they operate.

This is not a unique misapprehension concerning the workings of our sense organs, although perhaps it is an extreme one. Another example also involves the sense of hearing. How do we know where a sound is coming from? Sometimes we see the source and are thus informed of its position, but everyone is able to locate the origin of an unfamiliar sound heard in darkness, and usually with great accuracy. Sometimes we locate a sound source approximately by turning our heads until the sound is louder in one ear than in the other, but more often and with great precision we rely on the difference in the same sound as it arrives at the two ears. Consider for the present only one type of sound, a sharp click. The most important property of the bundle of sound waves constituting the click is the time of arrival of the first sound waves at the two ears. If the click comes from straight ahead, the two ears receive the first sound waves at exactly the same time because they are equidistant from the source. If, however, the click arises at some point to the right of the direction you are facing, it reaches the right ear a small fraction of a second sooner than the left. If the source is 90° to one side, the opposite ear is about 20 centimeters farther away than the closer one, and since sound waves in air travel about 30 centimeters per millisecond, this means that the maximum possible difference in time of arrival at the two ears is less than 1 millisecond. Yet such is the precision of the auditory portions of our brains that we can easily distinguish between a sound source that is straight ahead and one that is displaced only 10° to one side. If the source is 3 meters away, the 10° displacement which is clearly noticeable involves a difference in time of arrival at our two ears of about 0.1 millisecond. It is difficult

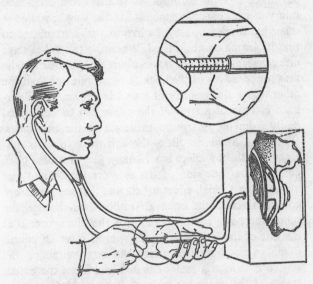

Fig. 15. Your ability to discriminate minute differences in the time of arrival of two sounds can be tested with this device. Any source of sharp clicks will do if it is tightly enclosed in the box so that you hear it only through the tubes.

to locate sound sources accurately if they lie directly in front of us, or anywhere in the plane that is equidistant from the two ears. If we have to attempt this, we usually do so by moving our heads about and bringing one ear closer to the source.

The role of differences in time of arrival of a click at

the two ears can be studied with the aid of a simple device illustrated in Fig. 15. This consists of a source of clicks, which could be a loudspeaker or a mechanical clicker, and a sound-tight box to house it. From the box lead two tubes each ending like a physician's stethoscope, but make sure the earplugs are soft to avoid accidental injury to your ears. One tube is fixed in length, while the other has a telescoping tube like that of a trombone so that its length can be varied. When the two tubes have different lengths, it will obviously require longer for the first sound waves of the click to reach one ear than the other. Since the velocity of sound is known, the difference in time of arrival of the clicks can be calculated easily from the difference in length of the two tubes. When one listens to clicks through these tubes of unequal length, the effect is strikingly like that of a click coming from one side. If the eyes are closed and one makes even a small effort to imagine that the clicks are coming through the open air rather than through the tubes, there is a compelling illusion that the source is at the side of the ear receiving the shorter tube. Of course it makes no difference where the box containing the source of clicks is really situated, nor does the actual length of the two tubes matter. When precise measurements are made with more refined apparatus of this same type, the minimum time difference that leads to this illusion of a source at one side or the other is less than 0.1 millisecond.

We need experiments like these to tell us about one of the principal ways in which we locate the source of a sound. We never think, "That click reached my right ear 1/10,000 second before it got to my left ear; therefore, it must have come from a little to one side of the median plane of my head." We simply recognize that the click came from one side without any idea how we located it. In much the same way, a blind man learns to anticipate collisions with obstacles under certain conditions, usually without realizing at all that these conditions are the presence of audible echoes. Recognizing the proximity of an obstacle and knowing from experience the pain of bumping into it, he comes to believe that he felt its nearness with his hands or face. All this adds up to a warning not to interpret the workings of our sense organs and our brains too hastily; they may be operating in other ways than we are first inclined to think. But we should not go to the other extreme and conclude that measuring instruments will always improve upon our unaided senses. As we have learned, sense organs and brains of men, porpoises, bats, and beetles accomplish extremely difficult feats of detection and discrimination.

To return to the blind man's problems of orientation, echolocation is certainly the technique by which skillful blind people find their way in the "dark." But with the general question thus answered, we are immediately impelled to ask what type of sound will provide a blind man with the most informative echoes. In the final experiments by Supa, Cotzin, and Dallenbach where the cart carried the loudspeaker and microphone up to the test obstacle, it turned out that a hissing noise was more effective than pure tones. But the average distance of detection was only 3.75 feet instead of 6.9. Does this mean that footsteps are more efficient sounds for this purpose, or does it mean that the cart with the loudspeaker and microphone was less easily controlled by the remote listener? From the experiments described in Chapters 2 and 3 it is clear that some sounds generate more useful echoes than others, and that a very short click has the advantage that it ends before the first echo begins to return. But footsteps on the floor are not especially sharp clicks, even when the walker's shoes have hard soles. Some blind men prefer shoes with metal heel plates, perhaps because of the sharper footsteps that result. If you have carried out some experiments with clickers, like the one illustrated in Fig. 7, it must be obvious that if you, a rank beginner, can detect trees, an experienced blind man can do at least as well. Many blind men have used clickers of one sort or another— aside from metal heel plates, the canes used by many blind men to lengthen the reach of their hands are used as clickers by tapping the ground or pavement. The resulting clicks provide a standard noise which gives a useful echo.

But we can properly ask whether footsteps, cane taps, or even toy clickers mounted in horns are really the best types of sound for a blind man's purposes. Do they generate the most informative possible echoes or are there other types of sound that would be superior? The question is simply asked, but the search for a convincing answer has been difficult and frustrating. Various types of clickers and portable sound sources have been built and tested. Some, particularly the directional clickers, have been used extensively by a small number of blind men, including their inventors. But the results have been far from satisfactory, and many users find it too difficult to hear consistent echoes or find the added facility at orientation not worth the embarrassment caused by a conspicuous audible sound that calls attention to their handicap. Yet almost every object that a blind man needs to detect does interact in some way with audible sound waves. This being so, why can we not devise a probing sound which will produce audible echoes that are recognizably related to the objects a blind man needs to locate?

One difficulty has already been called to our attention in the experiment where tape recordings of clicks or other impulsive sounds were played backward on a tape recorder. This experiment demonstrated the effectiveness of our built-in suppressor mechanism which renders echoes far less audible because our ears are temporarily insensitive immediately after a loud outgoing sound. A multitude of echoes are clearly audible on reversed playback when they precede a sharp click or pistol shot, but are quite unnoticed when they follow the louder sound as they do in ordinary life. Is this the major reason why blind men fail to learn as much from echoes as they theoretically should? And if so, could not some device be developed to overcome this difficulty? No one knows the answers to these questions, and they are good examples of the truism that no branch of science is complete or finished. Perhaps some reader may have the ideas and the opportunity to make further advances toward a real solution of the blind man's problems of orientation. Just because some men have failed so far to find such a solution, others should not be discouraged from new attempts, especially when the potential gains to human welfare are so great.

FURTHER READING

Barnes, H.: *Oceanography and Marine Biology*. London: George Allen and Unwin, Ltd., 1959.

This up-to-date elementary survey of oceanography includes a chapter on the sounds of marine animals and the use of sound for exploration of the ocean depths.

Boys, C. V.: *Soap Bubbles and the Forces Which Mould Them*. New York: Science Study Series, Doubleday Anchor Books, 1959.

A small readable classic of science which will give you, among other things, a better understanding of surface tension.

Bowen, E. G. (Editor): *A Textbook of Radar*. Cambridge, England: Cambridge University Press, 2nd Edition, 1954.

This textbook contains more general background material, including such fascinating subjects as radar echoes from the moon and the use of radar in navigation.

Buddenbrock, W. von: *The Senses*. Ann Arbor, Michigan: University of Michigan Press, 1958.

A readable and authoritative account of sense organs of all sorts of animals, from the eyes of scallops to inner ears of men.

Carthy, J. D.: *Animal Navigation*. London: George Allen and Unwin, Ltd., 1956.

This popular and readable book describes the orientation and navigation of insects, fishes, birds, and whales as well as those of bats and domestic animals.

Fletcher, H.: *Speech and Hearing in Communication*. New York: Van Nostrand, 1953.

This thorough and somewhat technical book summarizes the extensive researches carried out at the Bell Telephone Laboratories and elsewhere on the physical properties of speech, the mechanisms of human hearing, and the nature of hearing losses and deafness.

Griffin, D. R.: *Listening in the Dark*. New Haven, Connecticut: Yale University Press, 1958.

Many aspects of the natural sonar of bats, birds, and porpoises are discussed more fully than in this short monograph, including the many different types of bats and their orientation sounds, their pursuit and capture of flying insects, fish, and other food. There are chapters on echolocation by blind men, and on the acuity of echolocation achieved by bats, including their ability to hear faint echoes despite the presence of louder jamming noises.

Griffin, D. R.: "Bird Sonar." *Scientific American Magazine*, March 1954.

"More about Bat 'Radar.'" *Scientific American Magazine*, August 1958.

These articles contain excellent illustrations and supplement the chapters of this monograph dealing with the natural sonar of bats and birds.

Horton, J. W.: *Fundamentals of Sonar*. Annapolis, Maryland: U. S. Naval Institute, 1957.

This rather technical book describes the basic principles and operation of electronic sonar systems as they are used on ships. It explains the Doppler effect and other basic phenomena of echolocation with special reference to underwater sound.

Hurley, P. M.: *How Old is the Earth.* New York: Science Study Series, Doubleday Anchor Books, 1959.

This modern book on radioactivity as an energy source in the earth and as means of measuring time also includes a piece on seismic waves.

Pierce, J. R., and David, E. E., Jr.: *Man's World of Sound.* New York: Doubleday and Company, 1958.

A semi-popular book describing at an elementary level the physical properties of sound waves. It discusses such matters as interference, the propagation of sound, standing waves, etc., in a way which any student of secondary school physics should have little difficulty in understanding.

Ridenour, L. N. (Editor): *Radar System Engineering.* New York: McGraw-Hill, 1st Edition, 1947.

This is a general description of the radar systems developed during World War II by the Radiation Laboratory at M.I.T. While parts of it are quite technical, many chapters can easily be understood by any seriously interested reader of this monograph. Radar sets and systems are described and illustrated in sufficient detail to permit, for example, the sort of comparison with biological systems that were discussed in Chapter 5.

Rummell, J. A.: "Modern Sonar Systems." *Electronics* (Engineering Edition), January 1958, pages 58–62.

A brief survey of the apparatus used in sonar systems.

Witcher, C. M., and Washington, L.: "Echo-Location for the Blind." *Electronics,* December 1954, pages 136–137.

A brief but complete description of one of the more successful sound-generating devices used by blind people to find their way about. The late C. M. Witcher was himself blind and he devoted his engineering talents to improving such devices for his own use and for the benefit of other blind people.

Zahl, P. A. (Editor): *Blindness.* Princeton, New Jersey: Princeton University Press, 1950.

A collection of articles by different authors discussing the most important problems faced by blind people, education for the blind, vocational rehabilitation, talking books, guide dogs, guidance devices, and the remote possibility of direct stimulation of the optic nerves or visual areas of the brain.